I0607670

DEATH BRINGER JONES

ZOMBIE SLAYER

BOOK 1: THE BEGINNING
APRIL 2043 – APRIL 2044

THOMAS M. MALAFARINA

HELLBENDER
BOOKS

an imprint of Sunbury Press, Inc.
Mechanicsburg, PA USA

HELLBENDER BOOKS

an imprint of Sunbury Press, Inc.
Mechanicsburg, PA USA

NOTE: This is a work of fiction. Names, characters, places and incidents are the product of the author's imagination or are used fictitiously, and any resemblance to actual persons, living or dead, business establishments, events or locales is entirely coincidental.

Copyright © 2021 by Thomas M. Malafarina.
Cover Copyright © 2021 by Sunbury Press, Inc.

Sunbury Press supports copyright. Copyright fuels creativity, encourages diverse voices, promotes free speech, and creates a vibrant culture. Thank you for buying an authorized edition of this book and for complying with copyright laws. Except for the quotation of short passages for the purpose of criticism and review, no part of this publication may be reproduced, scanned, or distributed in any form without permission. You are supporting writers and allowing Sunbury Press to continue to publish books for every reader. For information contact Sunbury Press, Inc., Subsidiary Rights Dept., PO Box 548, Boiling Springs, PA 17007 USA or legal@sunburypress.com.

For information about special discounts for bulk purchases, please contact Sunbury Press Orders Dept. at (855) 338-8359 or orders@sunburypress.com.

To request one of our authors for speaking engagements or book signings, please contact Sunbury Press Publicity Dept. at publicity@sunburypress.com.

FIRST HELLBENDER BOOKS EDITION: October 2021

Set in Adobe Garamond Pro | Interior design by Crystal Devine | Cover design by Lawrence Knorr | Edited by Lawrence Knorr.

Publisher's Cataloging-in-Publication Data
Names: Malafarina, Thomas M., author.
Title: Death Bringer Jones, zombie slayer : book 1 : April 2043 – April 2044 / Thomas M. Malafarina.
Description: First trade paperback edition. | Mechanicsburg, PA : Hellbender Books, 2021.
Summary: In the mid-21st century, earth has survived the zombie apocalypse. Hero Death Bringer Jones recounts his exploits during the height of the plague.
Identifiers: ISBN 978-1-62006-883-0 (softcover).
Subjects: FICTION / Science Fiction / Apocalyptic & Post-Apocalyptic | FICTION / Dystopian | FICTION / Action & Adventure.

Product of the United States of America
0 1 1 2 3 5 8 13 21 34 55

Continue the Enlightenment!

For my wonderful wife, JoAnne.
Although as a writer, I'm supposed to come
up with the right words for every occasion,
I can never seem to find words enough
to thank you for your love and support all
these years as I go from one bizarre
horror writing project to the next.

INTRODUCTION

In 2013 I got an idea for what was supposed to be a once-and-done zombie novel. It was to take place in 2053, ten years after a zombie apocalypse at a time when humanity had beaten back the zombie hordes and society had rebuilt to the point where life was somewhat back to normal. Zombies still existed outside of the protective walls of the fortified cities in the wilderness known as the outlands. The book's name was Dead Kill, the title coming from the name given to a bounty placed on the heads of all zombies; a reward for killing something already dead.

I won't go into the book's details as you can read it yourself some time at your leisure. Suffice it to say, as I was writing the book, I realized it wasn't going to be the single novel I thought it would initially be but would be a series of books instead. As such, I changed the book's name to *Dead Kill Book 1: The Ridge of Death*; the word ridge being a play on the unwilling hero of the series, Jackson Ridge, a freelance writer and reporter. The book was published in May of 2014 through Sunbury Press.

In October of 2015, we published the second installment of the series, entitled *Dead Kill Book 2: The Ridge of Change*. As I write this, I've completed book three of the series to be called *Dead Kill Book 3: The Ridge of War*. For the record, I have no idea if the Dead Kill series will end with Book 3 or if there will be more. I tend to let things happen without any preplanning; life is much more interesting that way.

In *Dead Kill Book 2: The Ridge of Change*, I introduced a new character named Death Bringer Jones. He is a former zombie slayer, a folk legend who had once been famous and even depicted in pulp graphic novels. However, with the undead no longer a threat, he had found himself working as part of the Dead Kill cleanup road crew, a menial, low-paying job requiring workers to go around in trucks picking up the carcasses of Dead Kills. Unknown to me at the time, I would eventually find myself so captivated by the character that I found I wanted to write more about him during his glory days, the ten years preceding the Dead Kill series. I thought it would be cool to chronicle his life from the start of the apocalypse through the Zombie Wars and show how he evolved into the legendary character he eventually became.

So, I decided to start another series, Death Bringer Jones, Zombie Slayer. Yeah, I know what you're thinking; another zombie series from the guy who once said he'd never write a zombie story. Now you understand why I never plan and, more importantly, why I try to avoid saying never. (You'll notice I didn't say "never say never"). Absolutes are the bane of creativity.

I wanted the Death Bringer Jones series to be action-packed and full of good old-fashioned zombie-killing gore. I hope you enjoy this first book in my new series. Will there be more? I suppose time will tell.

Thomas M. Malafarina
October 2021

PROLOGUE

Delbert Bertram Jones here. God, I've always hated that name. Thanks, Mom and Dad. Wow! I can't believe I'm sitting down to write this. I suppose you could call these my memoirs. That seems sort of high and mighty for a regular guy like me. So, let's just say it's simply my way of telling you my story. Yeah, that sounds a lot better to me. At least I'll finally get to use that personal typing course I took back in high school. Even after all these years, I didn't forget what old Mrs. Grumbling feebly attempted to teach me. (More like force-feed me.)

I'll be the first to admit; this is all very weird for me. I'm not even sure why I'm doing this. I doubt if anyone even remembers who I am anymore, or I guess I should say who I was. This dilemma is especially true since I haven't been that person for several years now. It's strange to think that my name was something of a legend just a few short years ago. I suppose I should point out I'm not referring to my real name, Delbert Jones, but the name I went by then, Death Bringer Jones. Then again, you've probably already figured that out from the book title.

You have to admit Death Bringer is a pretty cool name, at least a hell of a lot cooler than Delbert Bertram. I stumbled upon that nickname accidentally, as you'll soon learn. Stumbling is pretty much how I've gotten through life so far. I was never one of those folks who had a plan for their lives. You know the type; graduate from high school, go to college, marry, buy a house in the burbs, have a mess of kids, then someday retire to Florida. Me? Not so much. Back in my younger days, people frowned on that lack of direction. However, in the end, having a life plan proved to be about as useless as lips on a frog.

Now back to me. After all, this account is supposed to be about me, right? Believe it or not, during the past decade, there were graphic novels and comic books printed depicting my adventures, that is to say, the tales of Death Bringer Jones. Although I must admit more often than not, the illustrator took the facts, stretched them to unbelievable lengths, and made everything seem larger than life. But then again, that's the purpose of such publications.

Today, in the year 2054, it's been eleven long years since the whole mess started. It's like this. At first, back in 2043, I was nobody, then for a while, I was the famous Death Bringer Jones, and now since about 2050 or so, I've gone full circle, and I'm back to being a nobody again. If that sounds a bit confusing, it's most likely because it is confusing. But such is my life.

If this isn't making much sense to you right now, I'll have to apologize for that. I can only hope it'll all come together eventually. You see, even though I'm not a dummy, I have no formal college education. Still, I like to think I have some limited skills as a writer. But trust me; I, unfortunately, won't be quitting my day job any time soon. I've always been an avid reader, however, so hopefully, that will prove beneficial. If my writing seems a bit less than professional from time to time, I'll have to beg your indulgence. I'll do my best to keep the tale flowing for both storytelling purposes and historical accuracy.

You see, I do have some incredible stories to tell, so who else could do a better job than me? After all, I'm the one who lived them and, in many cases, barely survived them. Maybe when this is all done, I'll have to turn it over to a professional editor for proofreading; that is, assuming I can find one still alive. Maybe I can snag someone from the local newspaper staff to check it out. I have someone in mind, a guy named Jackson Ridge. I knew him as a kid back when we both played ball, although I'm pretty sure he won't remember me. He's become famous for his investigative reporting.

By now, anyone still alive and reading this knows about the Zombie Virus of 2043, also known as the Z43 Virus. It struck without warning and was responsible for wiping out a large portion of the world's population. I won't bother to go into any lengthy explanation at this point but will do my best to fill in the details as my story progresses. That guy I mentioned before, Jackson Ridge, wrote a good book on the outbreak called "Dead Kill Book 1". It does a pretty good job of giving you an overview of the whole zombie apocalypse thing.

I have to apologize again. I don't know what the proper protocol is for this sort of storytelling or if I'm even explaining it the right way, so I guess the best thing for me to do is to just start at the beginning, back in 2043 on the night, which changed my life, and the world forever.

Delbert Bertram Jones
AKA Death Bringer Jones
April 2054

CHAPTER 1

APRIL 2043

Back before the outbreak of the Z43 Virus, I went by my given name of Delbert Bertram Jones. If you're interested, my parents named me after my paternal grandfather, Delbert Treadwell Jones, and my father, Bertram Thomas Jones.

Being saddled with a handle like Delbert Bertram, I chose to use the initials D.B. I found it made it much easier for me to avoid needless, random, and unmerciful beatings throughout the years from elementary through high school. My school had more than its share of mouth-breathing knuckle-dragging psychopaths. I wasn't a big guy back then and had little or no muscle tone. I also didn't know anything about fighting. I did, however, learn to excel at running, and my hiding skills were exemplary. I also learned on many unfortunate occasions that curling into the fetal position during a beating was an excellent way to protect some of my vital organs.

I also wasn't one of the best students or even one of the most mediocre for that matter, but I did somehow eventually manage to graduate my sorry backside from high school. But as I mentioned earlier, I had no real plan for how I would subsequently live my life. So rather than wasting my time and my parents' money going to college, I chose to enter the wonderful world of minimum wage retail employment. To say my folks were disappointed with my life choice would be the greatest of understatements. It may not sound very ambitious to you either, but I realized it was the only option for a first-rate underachiever like me.

As a result, on the evening when, as I like to say, the world went to Hell in a handbasket, I was just another regular working stiff doing my best to scrape together a meager living. I was working as a "Customer Service Associate" for one of the many big-box department stores in business during that time. The place was called Meggo Mart, and they had like a gazillion superstores around the world. Our store was just one drop in an ocean of stores, and I was just a tiny part of that drop. The fancy job title, Customer Service Associate, meant they paid me two dollars an hour over the minimum wage. Everyone else got minimum. For that vast sum of money, I had the pleasure of listening to the idiotic complaints of people who unbelievably were lower on the socio-economic food chain than even I was. My pitiful job was about a half step above what we used to refer to as a "do-you-want-fries-with-that" sort of gig.

To say my career choice at that time was painfully dull was another understatement, and to be honest, it was often more frustrating than most people would ever imagine, and here's the worst part. If you knew me back, then you'd know I was the sort of person who hated dealing with the problems of other people. You see, not only was it that I didn't care what other's issues might be, but it was also that I had plenty of issues of my own. Ok, so maybe I'm not speaking with complete honesty here. I was self-absorbed in my younger years. Then again, most young people are.

In addition, in those days, after having just survived the savage jungle that had been my high school, my first instinct was to distrust everyone. As a result, it took a lot to win me over trust-wise. As you may have figured out by now, this meant I was most definitely not in the right profession at that time. But it paid the bills, and truth be told, I was doing ok money-wise for a guy with no college degree and few, if any, marketable skills. Emphasis on the word ok; not bad or not great by any means, just ok.

For me, the absolute worst part of the job, which also happened to be the most critical part of my customer service job, was dealing with what I thought of as the "general public." I've often said all anyone needs to be considered part of that esteemed group is a pulse; no brains required, just a pulse, and I'm telling you, many of my most aggravating customers fit that description perfectly. Unscrew the top of their heads, then shout inside, and wait for the echo. I often thought of many of these people as brainless zombies. At that time, I had no idea how prophetic that idea was soon to become.

One of the few good things about my job, perhaps the only good thing, was that I worked the graveyard shift. Meggo Mart was open three-sixty-five / twenty-four-seven, and in case you weren't aware, working those hours meant I had to deal with what I thought of as the freakiest of the freaky. They were the people of the night. Ringling Brothers sideshow had nothing even close to the sorts of freaks I would encounter on a typical night in my store.

For example, I dealt with the goths with dark hair, black clothing, eye shadow, and black fingernail polish. Yeah, I realize it's hard to believe, but years after the fad faded away, they still existed. Hey, I suppose if you find a decade you like, stick with it. There were the gamers and geeks, the nerds and the stoners, the metalheads, the death metal freaks, the skateboarders, the wannabe rappers, the drunks, the bar hogs, and of course, the hookers. The world's oldest profession never dies.

After the clubs closed at 2:00 in the morning, I saw my share of what I was pretty sure were strippers. How did I arrive at this conclusion, you might ask? You be the judge. Visualize this; an overly busty, scantily clad woman wearing lots of makeup, and perfume, with traces of glitter on her clothing. She wiggles her way up to the customer service booth in a skin-tight leopard print dress to pay her store charge card with a stack of one-dollar bills. That's usually a pretty good indicator of her profession, at least in my less than expert opinion.

On quieter nights, I spent most of my time doing what I loved to do best. That was sitting at my customer service station reading sword and sorcery comics and graphic novels. They were awesome. While reading these books, I'm not embarrassed to say that I often imagined myself as some larger-than-life blade-brandishing hero. Even though I was about five feet ten inches tall and only weighed about a hundred and forty pounds soaking wet.

Don't get me wrong; it wasn't that I didn't try to do something about my physique. I tried lifting weights and eating fattening foods in a feeble attempt to build body mass, but nothing worked. One good thing about all that weightlifting was that I managed to become very strong in the process. I mean, you couldn't tell by looking at me because no matter how much I worked out or how strong I got, I still looked like a skinny little runt.

Hindsight being twenty-twenty, and in the name of complete honesty on my part, I have to admit I wasn't the best-looking guy back then either. My nose was sort of long; my eyes were a little too big and bulgy; I had what they call a weak chin, sunken cheeks, a patchy light mustache, and soul patch that was desperately trying to become a goatee. My Adam's apple tended to bob up and down along my skinny neck whenever I swallowed. Some people suggested I looked a lot like a much shorter version of the legendary Ichabod Crane, combined with the twentieth-century cartoon character Shaggy from Scooby-Doo.

I should also confess I was a bit on the lazy side, which is akin to saying someone's a bit pregnant. Ok, I was big-time lazy. I'm sure you can see how this contributed to the whole slacker attitude. Yet somehow, I figured the crappy job I had was just a bump in the road of life leading to my eventual fame and fortune. I often wonder how I could be so stupid as to think that by just sitting around wasting away in Meggo-ritaville, I would somehow become showered with wealth and notoriety.

I suppose in my slacker mind, I always assumed something would eventually come along to change the course of my future forever. As everyone who has lived knows, in life, no one gets anywhere doing nothing. Yet, I had this feeling. Again, I had no idea just how right I was going to be. However, back then, all I knew was that I was in a dead-end job in what was turning out to be a dead-end life, and I had no idea what to do about it. So as was typical of me, I did nothing.

Besides being a comic book superhero, a job for which I was nowhere close to being qualified, assuming such a profession existed, I couldn't think of any other position that would interest me. After my eighteenth birthday, I tried to enlist in the army, but these had been times of peace, and there was no need for someone as scrawny as I was. So, every branch of the armed forces turned me down flat.

The same thing was true when I attempted to get onto the local police force. I mean, seriously. It wasn't like I was trying to get into the state police or the FBI. I'm talking about but local town cops. I figured all these jobs were as close a superhero gig as I could ever hope to achieve, but they all rejected me, not that I could blame them, and for the record, I didn't even try to attempt the security guard or mall cop route. I didn't want to risk rejection from what I considered the bottom of the super-hero heap.

Instead, I sat behind the customer service counter drinking diet Coke by the gallons and reading graphic novels in between dealing with the hopelessly insipid problems of the great and mentally deficient unwashed.

Then one night, something unexpected happened. It was in the spring of 2043, April 15th to be exact, tax day. Without warning, the recently deceased began to leave their deathbeds by the thousands and started feasting on the flesh of the living. It was unbelievable! Like tax-day couldn't get any worse. Talk about adding insult to injury.

The long-prophesied zombie apocalypse had finally arrived. I'd been reading about it and watching it in movies and on TV for years. Now it was happening! But just like the government, police, and armed forces, I was caught entirely off guard. I think it was one of those situations when you know what's happening. Still, your brain refuses to accept it, looking instead for some alternate scenario, one that made more logical sense.

The night I learned about the Z43 plague, I was sitting in my usual spot behind the customer service desk reading my latest graphic novel, "*Blood of the Sword; Gore, and More.*" As I recall, the famous team of illus-trators, Chase Longbow and Rylan Waters, wrote that book. That's right, the same dynamic duo that developed the Krodon series back in 2030.

Anyway, I looked up from my book, and I noticed an odd-looking customer standing a few feet away across the counter from me; an old, bald dude. I immediately knew something was drastically wrong with him, but I had no idea what that might be. His skin was ashen, almost gray, and he stood in an awkward slumped position leaning to one side. It seemed to me that the very act of standing upright was a real chore for him. Ding, warning bell number one went off inside my head.

It looked to me like the old man was wearing pajamas. Strange as that may sound, seeing people shopping in their PJs wasn't an unusual occurrence for many of my late-night clientele. I had probably seen just about every sort of get-up imaginable on my shift. If you have any doubt, when you have a spare moment, check out the "People of Meggo Mart" website if it's still out there. You'll see examples of what I'm saying. But this guy's pajamas weren't what I thought of as typical PJs. They were a pale turquoise green color and seemed to be the sort of thing you might wear as a patient in a hospital. "Ding ding" warning bell number two.

The skinny old-timer just stood there staring slack-jawed at me, and he was moaning, or maybe he was even growling from somewhere way down deep in his throat. His eyes had this vacant, empty look, coated with a gossamer-like film as if he had cataracts or something. My grandmother had cataracts one time and looked a lot like this old guy looked. It was weird, even for Meggo Mart. To me, it seemed like he was looking at me but not seeing me at the same time. Does that make any sense? Maybe not, but that's the impression I got. There was also this steady stream of reddish-brown drool coming from the corner of his tilted mouth. Ding, ding, ding baby.

All sorts of alarm bells started going off in my head, and I immediately pressed the button under my service counter, signaling for security. It wasn't that I didn't think I could handle the old-timer on my own. I told you I was a pretty strong guy. But as far as I was concerned, even at the extra couple of bucks an hour, they didn't pay me enough to deal with this sort of freaky hassle. That was a job for security. I was grateful I'd chosen to skip trying to go the security guard route. I mean, who needs crap like this?

Speaking of security, typically, there was no in-store security for the night shift. But with all the recent reports of Braino addicts running loose in the area (that Braino is nasty stuff), the store had chosen to add an evening security guard of sorts. Granted, the jerk they hired for the position wasn't much of a guard and didn't exactly make anyone feel very secure. Why do I suspect no one is in the least bit surprised by this revelation?

Our resident security superhero was a gentleman named Harley Towson. Although he was a large man, well over six-foot-three, his more than three hundred and fifty pounds was all flab with absolutely no muscle tone whatsoever. That is unless you we're to assume his muscles might be safely hiding somewhere beneath the thick insulating layers of fat. He did his best to look more formidable than he was by shaving his head, growing a thick beard, and sporting more than his share of tats.

He seemed to eat constantly, which would explain why he didn't seem to have enough time to brush his rotting tombstone teeth. Most of my coworkers called him Harley-tosis because of his foul breath, which seemed to become magnified by his labored breathing and constant wheezing. Maybe that was his real superpower. He could always breathe on any wrong-doer and kill the villain with his breath.

I had no idea how long it was going to take Harley to get his fat butt over to my side of the store, so I decided to try to talk to the strange old-timer to see either what he wanted or, at the very least, figure out what the hell was wrong with him.

"Um, yes, sir, how may I help you?" I asked as warmly as possible, using my best customer service representative voice, the one I learned during my two-hour orientation class. Hey, formal training is vital for a job as prestigious as mine was.

The man just stood there gawking at me and then began slowly shuffling closer to the counter. I took an involuntary step backward and felt a cold chill race down my spine. There was something very wrong with the old codger. As I suggested earlier, I believe I knew even then what the situation was, but my mind kept coming up with more rational explanations. I hoped the gazillion security cameras mounted all around the store were getting good images of the guy for future reference. I didn't know exactly why at the time, but I had a definite feeling this encounter wasn't going to end well.

"Sir? Is there something I can do for you?" I tried again, feeling more uncertain by the minute.

The weird old guy lifted his right hand and brought it down hard on the counter surface with a terrible smacking sound. Then he opened his mouth and let out a loud, horrifying, blood-curdling howl. You know we've all heard that term "blood-curdling" but probably never gave it much thought. I'm not ashamed to say I now know exactly how that feels. It made the hair on the back of my neck stand on end. I might have always wanted to be a superhero, but truth be told, I wasn't even close back then. The guy weirded me out to the point of being damned terrified.

As if that howl wasn't bad enough, a God-awful stench accompanied his roar. That disgusting reek traveled across the short distance between the old man and me, and I thought I was going to hurl from the stink for a moment. I was notorious for having a weak stomach, and this dude's stench was pushing me to my limit.

"Good Lord, hadn't this guy brushed his teeth in like a month?" I wondered to myself.

His breath reeked even worse than Harley's did, and that's saying something considering Harler's breath smelled like he ate most of his meals from a ceramic bowl, one with a lid, and a handle, if you get my drift. That may sound disgusting, but the stench from that old man was like something I smelled once walking along a highway on a hot summer day and coming upon a bloated dead groundhog lying along the side of the road. Harley's breath came close, but this guy had him beat hands down, and speaking of Harley, where the hell was he, anyway?

Then just as I took another step backward, the man reached both hands across the counter, trying to grab me.

"Whoa there, Chester. You might want to lighten up a bit," I said. I was still hoping to find some way to talk my way out of this situation. I had gotten pretty good at fast-talking my way out of plenty of potential beatings in the past. But I couldn't seem to come up with any apparent pearls of wisdom to use on this character. He seemed to be way beyond reasoning anyway.

The weirdo was still doing that horrible growling, moaning thing, and drooling thick reddish-black gunk all over the counter. It was disgusting. That, combined with that awful smell, was making me feel like tossing my cookies. Why I hadn't barfed my guts out already, I didn't know. Then just when I thought I couldn't hold my dinner down any longer, I heard the sound of one of the electric guest carts coming around the corner, Harley to the rescue.

These special handicapped guest carts were only supposed to be used by customers with disabilities, but because Harley was so fat, he had to use one of them to get from one side of the store to the other. Otherwise, he'd likely not arrive until after the crisis was over, or else he'd probably drop dead of a heart attack along the way.

I always liked to call these motorized buggies "lard carts" because, more often than not, they weren't used by the genuinely handicapped but were driven around by fat lard-asses who, in my opinion, were too lazy to get off and walk around the store. I often wondered if being a fat tub of Crisco allowed them to be considered handicapped. I didn't think so, but that was a problem for store management to deal with, not me. It was way above my pay grade.

As the cart approached the counter, I heard Harley shouting at the old geezer in his typical gasping voice. "Hey! (wheeze). Hey you! (wheeze) Numbnuts! What the hell (wheeze) do you think you're doing?"

Ok, so maybe tact and finesse were two concepts beyond Harley's comprehension. But I supposed that sort of thing went with the job. It was an unspoken understanding that someone called for the cavalry; there was a severe emergency, and the time to be polite had come and gone. But still, referring to a customer as "numbnuts" might be a bit over the top, even for Harley. Then again, management's concern is not mine.

Harley wore his typical uniform, fat-man jeans; you know, the soft, stretchy kind with an elastic band. I suppose I should be grateful he didn't wear jogging pants or some other drawstring pajama-type things. God knows I'd seen my share of those in the store. He also wore a black leather vest over a black tee-shirt rather than the store-issued light blue vest like I had to endure. It had a gold pin reading "SECURITY" positioned predominantly above his left breast pocket. I had a feeling Harley may have made the pin himself as it looked like he had taken an empty plastic transparent visitor's badge and cut the letters spelling SECURITY out of a magazine. It bore a creepy resemblance to a ransom note I'd once seen on a TV crime show.

He sported a series of tattoos snaking up both of his forearms. Management allowed this indiscretion because they felt it helped to make him look more intimidating, which I suppose they hoped would compensate for his overabundance of flab. Harley was a scary-looking dude, and I

suspect this look helped him avoid a lot of potentially physical altera-
tions. It didn't matter if he was a rough character or not; the borderline
psycho look did the job most of the time.

I would never have believed it was possible, but with surprising agil-
ity, Harley jumped off the cart and shuffled, huffing and puffing toward
the counter, where he grabbed the old man tightly by his scrawny left
arm. I thought for certain Harley might snap the guy's arm like a twig.
Harley stood several heads taller than the old man and was like three
people heavier. But the old dude appeared unfazed by Harley's threatening advance.

"Hey, old man! (wheeze) I think maybe you'd better, (wheeze) back
off." Harley was one of those big guys who, for whatever reason, found
himself cursed with a high-pitched, almost child-like voice, which did
little to enhance his performance in the security guard arena. I think he
would have done better to project a strong, silent, and menacing image.
The voice, combined with the wheezing, didn't quite work for me.

Harley strained as he leaned down to get his face just inches from the
old man's face, staring angrily into his filmed-over eyes. I strangely began
to wonder if this turned into a bad-breath competition, which of them
would puke or pass out first. Yeah, I know that was a ridiculous idea to
have at that moment in time, but that's how my brain works.

With as much menace in his high-pitched voice as was possible, Harley said, "We don't (wheeze) tolerate this sort of crap (wheeze) in our
store, old-timer. Capish?"

The man stared seemingly uncomprehending at Harley for a second
or two, then without warning, he launched himself upward and sank his
teeth deep into the fat man's meaty throat. The old guy pulled himself
away from Harley and tore out two-thirds of the guard's neck. It was beyond gross, spewing a fountain of gore all over the floor of the customer
service alcove.

Then the old geezer snapped his head to the left. His dentures flew
out of his mouth and skidded through a blood pool and across the floor.
In a different situation, the sight of those choppers sailing across the floor
might have been hilarious. However, there was nothing even remotely
funny about it that night. Harley screamed in shock and pain, although

the scream caught in his throat, sounding very liquidy. It was enough to make my toes curl.

As he stumbled backward, he caught the heel of his right shoe on the front tire of the lard cart and fell to the floor, writhing and squirming in an ever-spreading puddle of blood. His tee-shirt, which was way too small for him, and which he never tucked into his pants, slid up, showing his massive stomach flab.

The old man threw himself down on Harley's mountainous gut and dug his long, yellowed fingernails deep into the fat of Harley's belly. His skinny hands disappeared up to his wrists in the big man's flab. A moment later, they withdrew full of intestines dripping with blood. The geezer let the innards slither between his gnarly fingers. The red liquid rolled down his wrists and up to his arms like grease from a pizza. Then he began to gnaw on the fat man's guts, oblivious to the fact that he was doing so with now toothless gums.

I felt a scream catching in my throat as I watched the horror unfolding on the floor in front of me. Try as I might; I couldn't control what happened next. I turned and spewed my dinner all over the floor behind the service counter. When I finished heaving and trying to regain my control, I stumbled to my feet on trembling legs and dared a glance over the counter.

I had no desire to see any more of the gory scene than I already had, but I needed to find out if there was any way for me to escape. I stood trapped behind the counter, with a solid wall behind me and the stench of fresh barf surrounding me. The only route out was to head into the store. I saw the old dude still deep in his feast of flesh ala Harley and decided now might be my best time to try to sneak away.

I hurried as silently as possible around the side of the service counter, staying as far away from the horror as I could. I had no idea what was wrong with the old-timer, but he was a bit more than crazy. I mean, cannibalism, even for a wacko, is way over the top. I did my best to avoid the area and made it to the central aisle of the store. I grabbed for my Communications Unit and dialed the emergency 911 number. But as rotten luck would have it, I got a busy signal. This night was certainly not shaping up to be a good one for yours truly.

I tried several more times to get through to 911, but I was never able to connect. So, I decided to make a break for the north entrance of the store. Once I got to the safety of my car, I figured I could always drive to get help. Here's the part of my story where I remind you that I wasn't courageous back then and, as I said, was also a bit self-centered. Ok, a lot self-centered. I wasn't thinking about the other workers in the store. The only thing I was considering at that time was how best to get my sorry butt out of there as quickly as possible. As things turned out, that wasn't going to be an option.

Standing across the wide aisle blocking my escape route were three other people of varying sexes and ages, all behaving like the lunatic who had just killed Harley. They were all wearing the same kind of light green pajamas the old coot was wearing. Then it suddenly occurred to me. All these weirdos must be escapees from some hospital or mental institution. I had once heard that there was a nuthouse in Danesville, a town about twenty miles away, but I wasn't sure. Maybe they were being transferred somewhere, and their bus crashed, releasing this hoard of crazies out into the general population.

I decided, for now, it didn't much matter who these wackos were or how they had gotten here. The point was they were here. So, I did a one-eighty and beat feet toward the South exit, but I had to stop in my tracks again. That original old man, now with his formerly green PJs covered in crimson gore, was lumbering toward me. As if that wasn't bad enough, I saw something which caused me to nearly crap in my drawers. Harley, yeah, that Harley, the dead one, was now crawling on his hands and knees along the polished floor right behind the staggering old monster.

"Hold the phone!" I thought! How could that even be possible?

I was certain Harley had been dead. For Pete's sake, I'd seen the fat man's throat torn apart and his guts ripped out of his body. You don't get much deader than that. Yet there he was, crawling along the floor like a massive slug leaving a snail trail of ruby red behind him, and here's something freaky. His head was flopping back and forth like a bobblehead doll because his mangled neck could barely hold the thing up.

There was no way he could still be alive, yet there he was, moving. I realized Harley had become some sort of monster. He was like a vampire or zombie or something. Yeah, that's it. I had read the books and seen the movies just like everybody else. Whatever Harley was, he wasn't human anymore. I was sure about that. Harley was growling deeply, just like the old man had been, and those other three pajama-clad crazies. I suddenly realized I had forgotten all about those other three freaks!

Just then, I felt someone grab onto the back of my store vest, and I half-turned to see one of the three loonies tugging on it. It was a young guy about thirty years old or so, and his mouth, which was now just a few inches from my neck, was snapping open and closed like a piranha on crack. This whacko was trying to chomp me.

I ripped open the front of my store vest, sending the brass buttons flying in all directions, and slipped out of it just as the guy gave a final tug. He stumbled backward and slammed into the other two. The three of them spun around aimlessly, looking like bowling pins, trying to re-gain their balance. Once again, under different circumstances, the whole thing might have been funny. But as with the old dude and his flying choppers, there was nothing funny about it that night.

I turned and made a beeline for the back of the store. Then I headed straight for the sporting goods department. I figured if I were going to have any chance to get out of that store alive, I'd have to find something to use as a weapon. Unfortunately for me, the store had stopped selling guns and ammunition several decades earlier during the anti-gun frenzy of 2025. However, they still carried plenty of hunting knives, bows, arrows, and other sporting equipment, including baseball bats.

As I approached the counter of the sporting goods department, I saw the department clerk, Jim Walker, looking at me like I had just gone nuts. He probably had good reason. I suspect I must have looked even crazier than those wacky cannibals at the front of the store.

"What's going on up there, Delbert? I keep hearing all sorts of strange noises coming from the front of the store." I noticed his hand reaching under the counter as if he was feeling uncomfortable enough to call secu-rity. Good luck with that one, Jimmy old boy. Harley-tosis is a dead man walking, or I should say, crawling.

Trying to sound as sane as possible under such insane circumstances, I said, "I, I don't know Jim. I just don't know. There's a crowd of crazy people back there. Maybe they're escapees from a cracker factory or something. They're up there walking around in their pajamas. They attacked Harley and killed him."

"Killed him?" Jim asked as I noticed his hand slide out from under the counter, and his eyes dart down toward the glass-covered knife display cabinet.

"Yeah. One of the crazies bit Harley, and ripped his throat right out, then started eating his guts and stuff."

"What?" Jim exclaimed. "That, that's not possible, D.B. You haven't been . . ." Then Jim lifted his arm and pinched his thumb and forefinger together close to his lips, pretended to be smoking a joint, suggesting I might have been enjoying my breaks way too much.

"Hell no, Jim. I'm as straight as an arrow, and you won't believe what I have to tell you next either. After a few minutes, dead Harley came back to life, and what remained of him started crawling along the floor. He was trying to get me too."

"Jeezus Delbert! How in the holy hammers of hell could Harley get up and chase you if he was dead? That don't make no sense. Hell, even alive, Harley didn't have the energy to do that."

"I'm telling you, Jim, these people are nuts. They're more hyped up than a car full of Braino addicts. It's like they aren't even alive."

"You mean like zombies?"

"Yeah, Jim! That's exactly what I was thinking a few minutes ago. They're freakin' zombies! They gotta be. Our store is under attack by the undead."

"Don't be ridiculous," Jim said, "I was just screwin' with you, Delbert. There ain't no zombies. These freaks must be lunatics or psycho killers or something."

I tried again to explain, "I'm telling you, Jim. Harley just got killed by one of them, and then he started coming after me."

"Look, Delbert, it sounds like we don't have much time to argue about this now. We can talk about it later. If we're really under attack here, we have to defend the store."

"Screw the store, Jim. I just want to defend my butt and get it out of here pronto. You need to do the same. What can you give me?"

Jim reached under the counter and pulled out a large hunting knife about a foot long and several inches wide in a black leather sheath. It was awesome.

"Whoa!" I said, "That's cool. That'll be great for up close and personal," I said, sounding like I knew what I was talking about, even though I didn't. Then I heard several of the clothing racks a few aisles away shaking. The crazies must have become tangled up in the clothing. Regardless, they were getting closer. I put the knife sheath down into the back of my pants, leaving the handle exposed for what I hoped would be quick access.

I asked, "Do you have something a bit longer, like a baseball bat or something, so I don't have to get so close to them?"

"No, I don't think so. We didn't get our shipment for the summer yet, and most of our old stock is sold out. I do have a hockey stick or two, though. Would you like one of those?"

"Hell yeah!" I said, "I don't know squat about hockey, but I could sure put a stick to good use."

Jim pointed to the aisle behind him, and I headed that way, hoping to find a strong hockey stick. Just as I grabbed onto a stick that I thought would suit my needs, I heard a snapping sound followed by a swishing noise and then a "thwop" sound. I turned and saw Jim behind the counter with a compound hunting bow at the ready, reaching for a new arrow. I saw one of the freaks in the aisle, with an arrow sticking straight out of its chest. It wasn't bleeding and was still coming for Jim. I couldn't believe what I was seeing. Before I even had a chance to react, Jim let loose with another shot, which found its way right into the maniac's left eye before it exploded out the back of his head. The thing fell to the floor with a thud.

Jim looked over at me, not showing a whole lot of emotion, and said matter-of-factly, "Ok. You win. They're zombies all right."

Just then, two more of the ugly things found their way out of the maze of clothing and were staggering toward the sports counter. I raced over to one of the monsters, a middle-aged woman, and swung my hockey stick with all my might catching the zombie right under her chin, snapping her neck bone like a twig. The woman fell dead to the floor with her head cocked at about a thirty-degree angle. I couldn't believe what I had just done. I suppose the only reason I could do it was because I didn't take any time to think. I just reacted.

I heard another swishing sound and saw that Jim had shot an arrow at the third zombie of the trio, another male, striking it in the right shoulder. The creature kept coming.

"Aim for the head! Aim for the head, Jim. You saw the movies. You know the deal. You gotta kill the brain."

Before Jim had a chance to load another arrow, the creature grabbed him by his right arm and bit down hard on his wrist. A fountain of blood spouted upward from the wound, and Jim's hand hung limp and useless. He dropped the bow, and tried to bring the arrow down, and plunge it into the thing's skull with his left hand but didn't have the strength to do it. That was when the creature grabbed his other arm, pulled him over the counter onto the floor, then fell on him, and began gnawing his throat apart. This horror all took place in like three seconds before I even realized what was happening.

What I did next, I did once again without thinking. I brought the hockey stick down on the creature's skull, cracking it open like a coconut, spilling brains and fluid all over the floor, and succeeding in breaking the curved end of the hockey stick right off. A single long pole with a sharp pointed end remained; not very good as a club, but it was better than nothing. It was weird. At that moment, I had this strange thought of an expression my grandfather used to say.

Whenever he got something of little value as a gift, he'd say, "It ain't much, but it's better than a poke in the eye with a sharp stick.", and now, ironically, the weapon I held in my trembling hands was nothing more than a sharp stick. Ok, so maybe the irony is lost on some of you. I don't know; perhaps it was one of those location things; you had to be there to appreciate it.

I suddenly snapped out of my thoughts, recalling that there were at least two more of those hideous monsters roaming the store, that original old man and Harley. It was then I heard a deep moan and looked down at the floor to see the corpse of poor mangled Jim getting up on his left hand and knees and looking at me like the breakfast special at Maggie's

Restaurant in my hometown of Ashton. Jim's mouth was opening and closing slowly, and he was crawling toward me using his one good arm.

I looked at my broken hockey stick and did the only thing I could think of; I shoved it hard into Jim's gaping mouth, pushing it hard until it came out the back of his skull. I'm telling you right here and now, it was beyond disgusting. Then thankfully, zombie Jim collapsed to the floor.

"Sorry about that, Jim, old buddy," I said through a quivering voice as the hockey stick hung out of the front of his head, "You were always an ok guy to me, and you probably deserved better. But well, you know. Nothing personal."

Without another moment's hesitation, I turned and did what I should have done earlier; I dashed through the warehouse and out the back exit. I no longer thought about the unbelievable weirdness happening around me, nor did I give any thought to finding more weapons. I just wanted to get out of the store and back to the safety of my apartment ASAP. I needed a shower, a stiff drink, or maybe four, and if I was lucky, a good night's sleep. Although I doubted any rest would be mine that night. I decided I should check the news when I got home and see what the hell was going on. Whatever it was, I knew it was too way much for Delbert Bertram Jones, customer service associate, to handle.

CHAPTER 2

BACKGROUND

Unknown to the public, for the first several months of the outbreak of the Z43 virus (Zombie virus on 2043), the government had been in denial. These events all took place before the official date of April 15, 2043, which is often called Z-Day. They refused to confirm scattered rumors suggesting the dead were returning to life. As a result, they did everything in their power to refute any such stories. Instead, they chose to blame the alleged zombie reports on the rampant use of a relatively new designer drug known as Braino.

Braino was the street name for a drug only in existence for the previous fifteen years, becoming internationally known a year or two before the plague hit. It was a highly addictive synthetic drug derived from crack cocaine, and heroin combinations, and several other highly addictive components. Braino got its nickname from the drain clog cleaner, Drano, because it did an outstanding job of cleaning out the brains of its users rather quickly, rendering them essentially mindless zombies. The drug ate its way through brain cells like Drano destroyed clumps of hair and other drain remnants.

Unlike actual zombies, Braino addicts often could be controlled and made to do the bidding of their handlers, but they, of course, had no natural craving for human flesh. In extreme cases of Braino addiction where the person had been high for several weeks, it would be difficult to tell the difference between the living addict and the undead zombie. But this fact wouldn't become public knowledge until it was much too late. Braino addicts also didn't move as slowly and lethargically as the reanimated dead did. However, because they moved much faster, they could often be more dangerous than a zombie. Even though these poor souls were not cannibalistic, if commanded by their handlers to eat someone alive, they might attempt to do so.

The denial by the government and their attempted cover-up was the main reason the zombie plague managed to catch humanity off guard. It was also why the virus had gotten such a significant head start. It wasn't until local authorities captured some of these so-called addicts that they discovered these creatures had no pulses or heartbeats, not to mention that they were in various stages of decomposition. This discovery was when they finally realized something else was responsible for their condition.

Still, not wanting to lose favor with their national government counterparts, local officials also chose to keep their knowledge about the appearance of zombies a secret from the public. But eventually, things had gotten so far out of control there was no longer any way to keep a lid on it.

On that fateful night in 2043, the world's people learned almost simultaneously that the dead indeed were reanimating and eating the living. Unfortunately, hundreds of thousands of people like Delbert Jones had to find out the hard way. Most of them didn't survive their first encounter with the creatures but instead were overtaken and became part of the growing numbers of the undead.

CHAPTER 3

I threw open the back door behind the warehouse. It slammed hard against the outside wall with an echoing bang as I ran for my life from the former Meggo Mart store, now turned slaughterhouse. I could hear the ear-piercing alarm screaming behind me. It was so loud I wondered if half the county could hear it. I had used the emergency fire exit for my escape. If that alarm brought police and the fire department, then all the better. I wouldn't have cared if it summoned the Marines; in fact, I wished it had.

I still had only the slightest idea of what had just happened to me inside that store. I mean, so much weirdness had happened so fast. I needed to find out if this was a local problem or if this insanity was going on everywhere. I was still having trouble wrapping my mind around what I'd just done. I wondered if it were true that I had destroyed a bunch of zombies. Me? Skinny, little, nonviolent, mind-his-own-business Delbert Jones? The idea was more bizarre than the plots of any graphic novels I enjoyed reading so much.

Then I suddenly realized what was happening that night was exactly like something out of an old comic book from the early part of the twenty-first century. I remembered reading how back around 2013 or so, there was a significant zombie fad in the horror world. It seemed like everyone had suddenly started loving all things zombie, zombie books, zombie movies, zombie TV shows. It was amazing. If it walked and was dead, people embraced it. The love of zombies was everywhere.

But like all fads, that one eventually wore out its welcome and faded into obscurity. I had all but forgotten about that zombie craze, and with good reason. I hadn't even been born until long after the fad had fizzled. But the more I thought about it, what had just happened inside his store was very much like what I recalled seeing in those old zombie books.

I had read a few of them back when I was a kid and didn't have much interest in them. I've always been more of a sword-swinging fantasy and superhero sort of guy. I always thought the zombie stories were boring and all similar. I mean, how much can you say about cannibalistic undead creatures shambling around killing and eating the living? Then surprise, surprise, if the dead dudes weren't too mangled, they'd rise back up to become zombies themselves, just like my boys, Harley, and Jim had done. They may have been dead, but they still came back.

However, now that I'd experienced it up close and personal, I could scarcely believe it had happened. Those creatures in the store had been zombies. Just then, I heard a loud banging sound, almost like an explosion, and the blaring door alarm suddenly went silent. At that exact moment, all the lights in the parking lot went out. Wonderful! I realized what had happened. An electrical transformer must have blown somewhere nearby. Thank goodness the moon was bright enough to provide at least some light so I could travel along the side of the building. I made my way carefully toward the front of the store and my waiting car.

In the quiet night, I could hear sounds that were in no way typical of the sounds I knew. Somewhere in the distance, I heard what sounded like hundreds of sirens blaring simultaneously. I heard ambulances, fire trucks, police cars, rescue vehicles, you name it, and what was even worse, I heard horrible screaming not only far in the distance but from nearby as well.

I cautiously worked my way around the corner, keeping my back tight against the building. If there were any more of those horrible creatures creeping around here in the dark, I didn't want them sneaking up behind me. I stayed hidden in the shadows and could see that the darkened parking lot only had a few cars. The moon was glimmering off their windshields. I knew my car was one of them. I looked out in the distance beyond the parking lot and could see the town of Franksville where I lived, which appeared to be on fire. Then I realized it wasn't just one fire but several large fires burning at the same time all around the town. Now, what was going on?

Suddenly I heard a mournful cry and saw a man of about fifty over-powered by three of the horrible creatures. Nearby a woman, I assumed his wife was hiding, huddled in the shadows just like I was. I figured she must have been paralyzed with fear. She was helpless to stop the creatures from devouring her husband.

I had no desire to get involved in anyone else's troubles. God knew I had experienced plenty of my own that night. I just wanted to get home safely. Was that too much to ask? Regardless, I guess, like in the store, I just reacted. I threw caution to the wind, and like a raving lunatic, I charged right into the group of zombies.

As I approached them, I reached around to the small of my back where I had tucked the huge hunting knife Jim had given me. I pulled it out and, swinging it in a broad arc, drove it into the ear of the first zombie I encountered. The blade sunk deep into the thing's brain. The squishy sound the knife made almost made me puke again, and it was even worse when I tugged and yanked out the blade because it was puss-covered with bits of gray matter stuck to it.

As things turned out, I got lucky. I had attacked the creature who not only was the one closest to me, but it was also the biggest and most formi-dable. This beast was a large and muscular male, while the other two were small, lightweight females. Without wasting another second, I dragged my blade across the throat of one of the female zombies severing its spinal cord and practically decapitating it. To be honest, I was shocked at how easily the blade had passed through the spine. The creature fell to the asphalt dead; its head twisted at a ninety-degree angle to the rest of its body.

The second female paid me little attention as she was busy chewing the flesh from the arm of the man who had now stopped screaming and with either unconscious or dead. Then suddenly, she twisted her head around and looked right at me. As she did, she peeled away a long strip of the dead man's musculature. It was beyond disgusting. I had to do something to make it stop. So, I shoved the blade into the woman's eye socket and just as quickly pulled it out. It made this sickening squishy sucking sound. I flicked my wrist, and the creature's blood and brain gunk slopped onto the blacktop. The dead thing collapsed to join the others in a heap. For a rookie, I was getting pretty good at this.

Next, I heard another low growl and knew I'd was wrong about the victim's wife. She hadn't been cowering in the shadows stricken with terror. No, this was something much worse. As I stood with my blade, still coated with slimy crap from that other walking cadaver, I saw the creature crawling out from the shadows. I could see all that remained of the woman was a head, a torso, and two arms: nothing else. Everything below the waist was gone, obviously some other creature's midnight snack. Still, the hideous creature kept crawling toward me.

I flipped the knife in my hand so the blade pointed downward, and I could tightly hold the handle in a two-handed grip. Then I plunged the blade deep into the creature's skull and stopped the thing cold. I tried pulling the knife out of the head, but it wouldn't budge. It was caught on something, most likely the thing's skull bones. I have no idea why I didn't scream, puke, pass out, or all three.

Instead, I put one foot on the dead zombie's head, and although I tugged with both hands desperately trying to pull the blade free, it remained snagged. Meanwhile, just a few feet away from me, the creature's recently dead husband, if it had been her husband, was growling and slowly trying to crawl toward me, just peachy.

As I struggled to get my blade free from the woman's skull, the other creature crawled ever closer, and man, was he ever disgusting. The thing was missing its right eye, right ear, and most of the right side of its face. It only had use of one of its arms while the other hung limp, dragging behind him. I didn't know if the thing could stand, but I doubted it since, like the woman, most of the guy's innards were dragging along on the ground behind him.

Finally, after a few more pulls, the blade came free. But I wasn't expecting what would happen. The force of pulling out the knife threw me off balance and almost knocked me off my feet. I felt like young King Arthur pulling the sword Excalibur from the legendary stone. That is, if the sword was a hunting knife, and the stone was a zombie's skull.

I decided I probably should try to skip that whole blade-through-the-skull thing again if I could avoid it. At that moment, all I wanted to do was get to my car as quickly as possible. I didn't waste any time destroying the crawling zombie. Instead, I kept my blade handy and used the parked cars and the darkness to give me enough cover to find my way safely to my car.

As I bobbed and weaved between the cars, I heard screams, cries, growls, groans, and pleas for help. I considered heading toward some of them and trying to help. But I was now entirely immersed in survival mode, so I chose to ignore them all. I figured if I were going to live through the night, I'd have to focus on one thing, and one thing only; that was getting my butt out of there.

When I got to my car, I practically fell behind the steering wheel and slammed the door tightly shut, immediately pressing the automatic door locks. For a second, I thought I heard a low growl coming from the back seat. I was sure I had remembered locking the car before work, but maybe I hadn't. With my left hand, I turned on the interior lights while at the same time I used my right hand to whip around with my knife, and I began slashing wildly into the back seat area. I had no idea if that would do any good, and I felt stupid afterward. But thankfully, the back seat was empty. I switched off the dome light and started the ignition.

"Wham!" I heard a loud noise coming from out of the darkness in front of my car. I could scarcely make out two shadows in the blackness. I turned on my headlights and saw two of the ugly-ass undead creatures standing directly in front of me, one leaning against the hood banging on it with its hands, and another a few feet further back but moving steadily closer. They were both older males. Their gray-filmed eyes seemed to glow in my headlights. I decided not to waste any more time than was necessary dealing with them, so I put my car in drive and pressed my foot hard against the accelerator.

I felt the car buck several times as it first ran over the closest creature and then the other. Looking in my rearview mirror, I saw I had run over one creature's head; I wasn't sure which one, flattening the lower part of its head like a deflated balloon and forcing what remained of its brains to squirt out of its eye sockets. The other creature lay on the ground writhing around with a broken back. Neither one of them was a threat to anyone anymore, so I figured it was time for me to make like a baby and head out.

I drove to the exit ramp and then toward the steep hill leading down to the town of Franksville. I started to wonder if my apartment still even existed, and if it did, would it become overrun by monsters? So much of the town seemed to be on fire. There were so many sirens blaring all at once; I had no idea how much of the city still survived.

CHAPTER 4

As you might have guessed, I drove like a maniac through the burning town, taking back streets and doing everything I could to avoid burning buildings and falling debris. I flew through traffic lights and stop signs hurrying to reach my apartment, and did so in complete disregard for speed limits. It sat at the back edge of town near a wooded area. At first, I thought the apartment's location might be a problem because of how long it took to get there. But as it turned out, being on the outskirts probably helped save it from the fires.

I rented a small, one-bedroom efficiency apartment above a two-car garage at the rear end of a property owned by an old lady, a widow named Mrs. Edith Willingham. It was one of only a hand full of single units in the borough. Most homes were wood-framed row houses. Since many of those houses dated back to the early twentieth century, few had firewalls. This structural condition was partly the reason for the large fires spreading throughout the town. Often when one rowhouse burned, all four or six units went up in flames as well. Sometimes entire blocks burned.

As I drove, I felt reasonably confident that my place would still be intact since the home was built toward the end of the twentieth century. The garage was also unattached and located a reasonable distance from the main house. The property was also far away from older row homes. But that didn't mean it was necessarily safe or secure.

Before I had made it to the side streets, I drove through the business district of town. I saw many people, humans, not zombies, looting stores and fighting each other in the streets. The city appeared to have been thrust into instant anarchy as people were beating each other senselessly for no apparent reason. I had always heard that in the face of a looming catastrophic event, civilization had the potential of self-destructing in a matter of hours, but I never believed it could be true. What I was witnessing made me a believer.

I saw one store owner I knew, a kindly older gentleman named Bill Kowalski, point a shotgun at a young man attempting to loot his jewelry store. Bill pulled the trigger, and I saw the young man torn in half by the blast. Kowalski looked over at my passing car and nodded his head in recognition. I could scarcely believe not only what I had just witnessed, but the store owner's calm reaction to it, like blowing some guy in half was just another day at the office. "Take this!" Kaboom! "Oh hey, Delbert, how are things with you?" Things were most definitely very different in this quiet little town, and I suspected they would be for a very long time to come.

That single surreal moment of eye contact and that creepy friendly greeting was so bizarre I could scarcely comprehend it, and to think it occurred just seconds after the killing. The man I believed to be a simple law-abiding merchant had blown another human being in two. It was like I was living in a nightmare; I went to sleep in my bed but woke up in that old TV show called the Twilight Zone from the twentieth century. The dead were returning; people were robbing and looting; others were fighting and killing each other in the streets. Where the hell were the cops?

I continued driving toward my apartment. As I turned the corner just a few blocks from home, I heard a woman screaming. Looking out the driver's side window, I saw a big guy on the ground straddling a young woman pinned under him. She appeared to be struggling to get free, but he was too powerful, and I knew she didn't stand a chance. The attacker was trying to pull down her pants as she screamed, realizing she was about to be raped and likely murdered.

Once again, I found myself questioning what I should do. Here was yet another obstacle to my progress. Should I ignore the conflict and drive on, or should I stop? Only yesterday, the most challenging problem I had was deciding whether to go to work or call in sick. In the past several hours, I'd seen the dead return to life and several people killed and eaten. I had killed, if you could call it killed, many of the horrible creatures myself.

Now I realized if I intervened on this woman's behalf, I'd likely have to either hurt or perhaps kill another living human being, not a zombie but a live person. I honestly didn't know if I could do such a thing. I didn't only mean because of the emotional stress of taking another human's life either. The guy was a bruiser. He had to be well over six feet tall, and his massive, tattooed muscles rippled below his wife-beater tee shirt. It was pretty much a given that he could break me in half without generating two drops of sweat. Yet, I knew I couldn't just drive by and do nothing. Could I?

Before I realized it, I had pulled my car over to the side of the street, had thrown open the door, and was heading toward the pair shouting, "Hey you, stop that!"

I had to admit my voice sounded as ineffective as Harley's had with the unfortunately high-pitched reedy quality it had back then. To make matters worse, I looked anything but physically threatening, especially with the short-sleeved white shirt and black pants I was required to wear on my job. I looked as deadly as a slightly disgruntled Jehovah's Witness. I was just thankful I still didn't have my store vest. Regardless, compared to the much larger, would-be rapist, I appeared anything but threatening.

The huge man turned to glare to find out who it was that had the nerve to interrupt his fun. He saw me and essentially ignored me, saying, "Get lost, little boy. I have man's work to do here. Maybe if you're a good little boy, I'll let you have sloppy seconds."

Oh, now that sort of derogatory comment was inappropriate. The ape was just trying to make me mad, and guess what? He succeeded. I pulled my knife around for the guy to get a good look and make sure he understood I meant business. I shouted, "I told you to let her go. Now, do as I say."

No sooner had the words left my big mouth than I realized my mistake. The dude was even more massive than I had believed he was. He stood up to his full height, and I could see he was well over six feet seven and rippling with even more muscles than I anticipated. It was no wonder the woman couldn't get free. I immediately understood that knife or not; I was no match for this man-monster.

While the man was focusing on me, the woman crawled backward, wriggling out of her jeans which the attacker's massive feet had pinned to the ground. Then she quickly stood, pulled up her panties, and ran off into the darkness. The huge man saw her flee but did nothing to try to stop her. I suddenly had a bad feeling about how this encounter was about to turn out.

He turned back to me and said, "Looks like you let my little prize get away from me, and to think, the girl was so young and so tender. Now, what am I supposed to do, little boy? Stand here with a major case of blue balls?" Delbert could see the enormous erection inside the man's bulging jeans.

"You know, little boy, back when I was in the joint, we didn't have us any pretty women like that one either. But you wanna know something? That didn't stop me from getting my ashes hauled if you get my drift. One of my favorite bitches in stir was a skinny little fella who looked an awful lot like you. Yeah, he was a real sweetie pie all right, soft in all the right places, and could that boy ever squeal just like a little stuck piglet! Come to think about it; you're gonna be a squealing sweetie pie piggie for me too. I'll enjoy making you squeal too. Yes, sir-ree, you'll make a perfect substitute for the one that got away."

Before this situation, my biggest fear that night had been trying to keep from being killed or eaten alive. I never even considered the possibility that I might end up being a love doll or human pin cushion for some shaved ape. I wasn't a big football fan, but it was clear that this maniac planned on turning this tight end into a wide receiver. Not only was this a possibility but a probability within the next few seconds.

"You stay right where you are, or I swear I'll cut you," I said, brandishing my blade in front of me and trying to lower my voice an octave or so. "I mean it. You stay back, or you're a dead man!" I honestly didn't think he'd buy my threat because I could scarcely believe it myself. But I had to do something before this guy decided to take my temperature rectally without a thermometer.

Of course, the thug didn't listen to my warning and attempted to step toward me with his muscular meaty arms extended. However, as it turned out, my luck was still holding on because the big man's feet became tangled up in the pants his intended victim had left behind, and like a mighty oak in a forest, he fell face-first toward me. His arms began to pinwheel at his sides as he struggled futilely to regain his balance.

I tried to step back to avoid the collapsing giant, but I still unknow-ingly had my hunting knife extended, pointing upward. Yeah, you guessed it. The tip of the blade entered the eye socked of the falling man. I immediately let go of it upon the realization. The knife's handle hit the pavement as the brute landed hard, driving the blade up and out the back of his skull. His body twitched once or twice, then lay dead on the sidewalk, a pool of crimson spreading out from under the corpse.

Staring down at the body, I could scarcely comprehend what had just happened—some force, luck, Karma, God, whatever had been watching out for me that night. To have survived so many encounters with the undead and now to have lived through this human monster's attack told me perhaps the universe had some higher purpose in store for me indeed. I couldn't imagine what that purpose might be, but I thought I'd find out sometime soon. But maybe those ideas were a bit too grandiose for a mere customer service associate like me, who pretty much just stumbled through life so far.

"You, you saved me," a small feminine voice said from out of the shadows. Moments later, the girl I had reluctantly and quite accidentally rescued came strolling out of the darkness. I could see she appeared to have calmed down a bit from when she had fled. I had assumed she'd run as far away from the scene as was possible. Then I realized she'd only run into the shadows where she waited until she felt it was safe to return. I wondered what she might have done if I had been caught and raped by the madman. Would she have remained hidden, watching and waiting until it was all over? I didn't want to think about that scenario. Then I realized she had just witnessed me killing a man. Accidental or not, I had killed another living human, and she had seen me do it.

As she approached me, I saw she was dressed only in a ripped blouse which she held partially closed with one hand. As the bottom of the shirt moved, I saw a pair of revealing pink bikini panties. She was barefoot. I had no idea where her shoes were or if she had ever had them. The girl shivered in the chill night air. I could see black lines of running mascara streaking her face from her tears.

I watched as she walked over to the body of the dead would-be rapist, and although barefoot, she kicked the dead man in the face with the ball of her foot, rolling his head over, causing the handle of my knife to point skyward. I thought I heard a cracking sound, perhaps the man's neck-breaking. My legs started turning to rubber, but somehow, I managed to hold on. Some hero I would be if I keeled over.

"Bastard!" She screamed at the corpse. I said nothing as I watched, unsure of what to do next. The girl reached down and pulled her jeans out from under the thug. She slowly slipped the jeans up over her long legs.

As she did, I asked with a stammer, "Are, are you alright?"

"Yeah. I suppose I am now," she said, "Thanks to you."

She looked around the body the bent down and picked up her shoes. Ei- chee Momma, she was one gorgeous babe. Once her shoes were on, she slowly walked over to me, and looking up at me with eyes still moist with tears, she put her arms around my neck and rewarded me with a long, deep, passionate toe-curling kiss.

After she pulled away from me, I noticed her blouse had slid open. To my astonishment, I could see she wasn't wearing a bra. A lump formed in my throat, and despite the horrors I had been through that night, I found myself suddenly very interested. Nature is truly a fantastic thing.

I stood still and speechless as she slowly backed away from me, never breaking eye contact and not making the slightest attempt to hide her exposed breasts. And yes, if I thought she was gorgeous before, I most certainly thought she was now. She gave me a sensual look, then asked, "And may I ask what the name of my brave and mysterious hero is?"

At first, I had no idea who she was talking about. I was busy gawking at those two rib balloons. Momma mia! Realizing I had better reply, I stuttered, "J . . . J . . . Jones. D . . . D . . . B . . . B . . . D. B. Jones"

"D. B. Jones, is it?" She looked down again at the corpse of her attacker. Then she looked at me and said, "So what does the D. B. stand for?"

I was about to tell her when she interrupted me, "I guess that it must stand for Death Bringer. Yeah, that's how I want to think of you, Death Bringer Jones, my special hero. You most certainly brought a well-deserved death to that horrible monster."

"But, but . . ." I managed to eke out.

The young woman smiled at me, patted my cheek, and said, "Stay safe, Death Bringer. I have a feeling we'll meet again. We're entering dangerous times, and it'll be good to know someone like you is out there watching out for people like me." With that, she turned and ran off into the darkness.

I stood dumbfounded for a few moments, uncertain what to do next. It all seemed surreal; then again, the entire night had become some unimaginable nightmare, so why would this be any different? Then I realized the only weapon I had to defend myself was embedded deep in the skull of the dead man at my feet.

"Great!" I thought with disgust. "Another blade stuck in a skull, and now I'm gonna have to wrestle it free." I really would have preferred to leave it where it was and even considered doing so. But I had just killed a man with that knife. He wasn't a zombie but a man. I had done so with a knife that had my fingerprints all over it. After a night of madness like we were experiencing, another dead body might not attract much attention. However, if somehow things got back to normal in a few days, I certainly didn't need a knife with my fingerprints discovered sticking out of the head of a dead man. My stomach lurched at the thought of what I had to do next.

With extreme revulsion, I placed the sole of my shoe against the dead thug's face and began tugging on the hilt of his knife with all my might, twisting it side to side as I did so. I could feel the corpse's nose cartilage cracking under the pressure of my foot, but I did my best to ignore the sensation. In my mind, I could imagine the crunching sound the crushed bones would make.

After a few moments, the blade broke free, and I yanked it from the skull. I turned to examine it to make sure it was still ok, and I saw the rapist's eyeball still clinging to the blade back by the hilt. I didn't need crap like that, not after everything I had been through that night already. I flicked the edge of the knife downward, snapping my wrist and trying to get the disgusting thing to fall off, but it remained embedded. I was on the verge of puking all over again. Regardless, I did what I had to do to remove the pierced orb. I grabbed the spongy feeling thing and slid it slowly back along the blade until it fell off the front, dropping to the ground and making an awful splat sound as it hit the pavement.

I could no longer hold back my disgust. So, I bent over and vomited for the second time that night, quickly ridding myself of what little remained inside me. Later, after a few minutes of dry heaving, I stood up and took a deep cleansing breath of cool but smoke-tinged night air. Some superhero I was. Death Bringer Jones, indeed. I probably should be given the name Barf Bucket Jones. I coughed a few times, returned to my 2025 Matsura Sedan, and drove the remaining distance to my apartment.

CHAPTER 5

I was surprised to find the area surrounding my apartment quiet and free from the insanity occurring in other parts of town. I thought about checking on my elderly landlady Mrs. Willingham in her nearby home, but it was the middle of the night, and all of her lights were out. So, I decided that it would be better to leave her rest as long as she was sleeping. The fires hadn't made it back to this part of town, and I doubted they would, at least for the night. I also didn't think I'd be getting any more sleep that night anyway, so I figured I could keep my eyes and ears open for any sounds of danger coming from her home. If so, I could always respond as necessary.

I opened the door to my apartment, and with my knife in my hand, I did my best to be ready for who-knows-what I might find inside. I flipped on the light switch and was surprised to see I still had electricity. I figured maybe this part of town hadn't been affected by the power outage yet, either. I closed the door behind me then quickly went from room to room, checking to make sure no invaders, living or otherwise, had been lurking. I walked back, secured the deadbolt on the front door, and then slumped into my recliner. I had to find out just how bad things were. Using my remote control, I turned on the television, switching to one of the all-news channels.

The picture displayed was grainy and flickered in and out of clarity, as did the audio. This poor broadcast consisted of a staccato assortment of partially interrupting words and pictures. It was almost impossible to decipher.

"... numerous reports ... in ... dead ... returning ... cannibalism," a harried-looking female reporter said as she stood on a darkened street corner with a microphone. What light they had must have been from spotlights run off the TV station's generator in the news van. The image was moving in and out of clarity, but I could see that the woman must have once been a natural beauty, a typical fashion model talking head, but not tonight. Now, she appeared haggard, frazzled, with little makeup, and almost no attention paid to her hair or wardrobe whatsoever.

"The National Center . . . Disease, and Virus Control . . . unexplained . . . dead . . . returning . . . eating . . . living."

I struggled to learn more, but it was useless. From what little I could determine, what happened to me at the store was happening everywhere. As I watched and strained to hear more, the audio cut out completely, leaving the sporadic image of the reporter standing there moving her mouth in silence. Then from the left side of the screen, I saw several people approaching the reporter. I instantly realized they weren't living people at all but were a cluster of zombies.

I found myself screaming at the telecast like an idiot, yelling uselessly for the reporter to watch out but, of course, she could no more hear me than I could make out what she was saying. The creatures fell upon the reporter and apparently must have gotten her cameraman as well because a moment later, the camera crashed to the ground but was somehow still working enough to keep filming. What I and the rest of the television audience saw that night would likely haunt our nightmares for as long as we were lucky enough to stay alive.

The woman struggled and thrashed; her silent screams nonetheless horrific as one by one, the undead creatures began systematically tearing strips of flesh from her body. One of the horrid creatures was on her face biting off her nose, then plunging its fingers deep into her eye sockets and plucking out the tender morsels before popping them into its drooling bloodied mouth.

Another had ripped off her blouse and had pulled down her bra, momentarily revealing her breasts before biting into them and tearing one completely from her chest. I knew I shouldn't watch such a horrible display of savage horror, yet I couldn't seem to take my eyes off the unholy carnage. Just as two other creatures were beginning to extract the dying woman's insides, the broadcast mercifully cut off. I didn't know if it was due to technical difficulties or if the station had cut the feed. Either way, I was grateful.

Moments later, the television screen went black. I searched with the remote for a few more minutes but saw nothing; not even the emergency broadcasting system seemed to be functioning. I clicked off the unit and sat for a moment staring at the blank screen, thinking. So much had happened over the past several hours. So much had changed. What was going on with the world? What was happening? Why were dead people returning, and why were there suddenly so many of them? Then I remembered over the past several weeks hearing scattered reports of acts of extreme violence; over the top stuff such as people killing and even trying to eat other people, but previously Braino had been attributed as the cause of all of those incidents.

I knew that Braino addicts could commit heinous and unspeakable horrors in the most extreme situations. In every incident I had heard about during the past months, the government and its medical agency, the National Center for Disease and Virus Control, reported there was absolutely no epidemic of violence taking place. The NCDVC suggested the incidents were nothing more than isolated attacks by a few wretched drug addicts.

But now I knew the truth. Something very wrong was going on. It had to be some sort of disease or virus. Maybe it was something spread through food, water, or air. Or perhaps the virus spread through saliva or blood, I didn't know. How could I possibly know? I was no doctor. I had no medical training whatsoever. I was nothing, just a customer service representative at a big box store who was now out of a job as far as I knew.

Yet, these ideas seemed to make sense to me. Perhaps it was because of all the comics and graphic novels I had read. Maybe it was the scores of sci-fi and horror movies I had watched throughout my life. Or perhaps it was nothing more than simple common sense. I seemed to understand not only what was happening but what would likely happen next.

Something was causing the dead to reanimate and eat the living. The reanimation happened only a few seconds after a living person died. I had seen that firsthand with my coworkers just an hour or so earlier. I sat wondering what I was going to do. I realized I had been running on pure adrenalin for the past several hours, and exhaustion was beginning to overtake me.

Suddenly the room was thrust into darkness; the power outage had finally reached my side of town. I wasn't about to go outside in the dark with all that was happening. I was sure I was as safe as I could be in my apartment, at least for a while. There wasn't much else to do but to catch up on my sleep. I didn't know what problems I'd face in the morning, but I was sure that a few hours of good shuteye could only help. I rested my palm on the handle of my knife, closed my eyes, and before I even realized it, I fell quickly into a deep exhausted sleep.

I woke up, hearing a loud continuous pounding on my front door as morning sunlight streamed into my living room. Although it did seemed a bit hazy, as if there might be storm clouds overhead. I awkwardly rose to my feet. My muscles ached. At first, I assumed the pain had been from sleeping on the chair all night. I realized the aches had likely resulted from the violent encounters I had experienced the previous evening.

The pounding continued. I shuffled over to the front door. As I did, I glanced out the living room windows and could see something was very wrong outside. There were still clouds of billowing smoke and flames coming up from rooftops. The fire was much closer now. The haziness I saw wasn't from cloud cover but the smoke. The town was still burning, and nothing seemed to have changed for the better since the previous night. Things had gotten much worse. The thumping on my door was relentless.

I yanked open the front door, and to my surprise, I saw my landlady Mrs. Willingham standing, and staring at me through what were now gray-filmed eyes. Her white hair was unkempt and stuck out in several different directions. She was typically a very proud woman and careful about her appearance, but that was no longer the case. I had never seen her in such a condition and, at first, didn't even recognize her. The thin cotton nighty she wore left little to the imagination, which, when considering her advanced age was nothing, I was in any hurry to see.

I was about to ask if she needed anything when my still drowsy brain began to comprehend that the thing standing in my doorway was no longer the woman I had known but an undead reincarnation of that once sweet old lady. The creature started to advance toward me, her slack-jawed mouth moving slowly open and closed as if in anticipation of a delicious meal. Unfortunately, the specialty of the house happened to be "Delbert tartare." I had no intention of allowing that item to stay on the menu; thank you very much.

She started toward me just as I slammed my front door closed. The swinging door struck Mrs. Willingham squarely in the face shattering her nose and popping out several of her brittle old teeth. But more importantly, the impact caused the undead woman to fall backward. She pitched over the second-floor railing and plunged to the ground, where her head struck the asphalt driveway and cracked open like a coconut spilling brain sludge out all over the blacktop.

I opened the door again and walked out to look down over the railing at the mess below. For whatever reason, I felt the need to apologize, "Sorry about that, Mrs. W. You were always a nice landlady. But, well, you know. I mean, after all, you were going to eat me."

I let out a deep sigh and looked out over the burning rooftops of the town, wondering what precisely this new day would bring. I shook my head in resignation and did the only thing I could think to do. I went back inside and re-locked my door securely.

CHAPTER 6

Walking back toward the bathroom, I stripped off all my clothes and got into the shower. The water coming from the showerhead was tepid since the electric water heater was no longer functioning. I did my best to get clean in the rapidly cooling water, knowing this might be my last opportunity to do so for a very long time.

I finished my shower in record time due to the discomfort of the water temperature, but I had no desire to waste precious water. I also realized I was going to have to fill many containers with fresh water for drinking. If the world were experiencing more of what I saw the previous evening, it wouldn't be long before fresh drinking water became an endangered and, therefore, valuable commodity.

I took every empty container I could find, filled them with water, and placed them in my bedroom closet. Once I had completed that task, I looked for something to wear. It wasn't that I cared about fashion, but to be honest, I wanted to find clothing that might make me seem a bit more intimidating. I wanted to make sure any living criminal types I might encounter didn't see me as an easy target. I realized I had only survived that encounter with the rapist by sheer bad luck on the attacker's part and didn't want to risk rolling that pair of dice too many times. I figured if I could look like someone not to be screwed with, then maybe I might be left alone.

In the bottom of my closet, I found a pair of gray snakeskin boots. I had bought them on a whim one day but never had the nerve to wear them, despite the ridiculous price I had paid for them, or maybe it was actually because of that cost. Buying them had seemed like a good idea at the time, but then in hindsight, I wondered what the hell I'd been thinking. Now they seemed like just what the doctor ordered.

I also found a pair of black leather pants in the closet, leftover from a very brief period when I had tried to be the lead singer for a local heavy metal band. The entire life span of the band consisted of about six months, two gigs, and about a million rehearsals. But now I saw another use for the leather pants.

I picked out a dark black cotton tee shirt with a skull on the front and, after some digging around, located the leather vest I'd bought to go with the pants. I dressed and stood in front of the mirror, examining the result. It wasn't perfect and seemed to be missing something, but I thought it would do for the time being. I wished, as always, that I had more muscle tone.

As I looked at myself in the mirror, I began to wonder what I had been thinking. Why should I even consider going outside? At least until I got a better understanding of what was going on in the world. It was ridiculous. Here I was worrying whether I appeared tough enough, like some high school girl trying to decide what to wear on a date with a boy I loved.

For all I knew, I could walk out the door, go down the stairs, and either have a bunch of those undead creatures eat me, or else some insane living human might rob or murder me. I was sure that by now, the entire world had probably gone crazy. I decided to stay right where I was for a while and see what the future brought. I traded the leather pants, vest, and boots for jeans and sneakers. I kept the tee shirt. I sat back down on my recliner, began to read, and wait. Unfortunately, I didn't have to wait very long.

Around noon, noises woke me. I hadn't realized I had dozed off again. At first, I heard screaming, then growling coming from outside. I got out of my chair and went to the window, careful to make sure no one could see me. My former landlady's home was in flames, shooting out from every window. I could see five people encircled by more than a dozen zombies down on the ground surrounding the property. The victims were being corralled back toward the burning structure. I doubted the creatures had the intelligence to herd their prey in such a way deliberately, but I assumed the monsters had surrounded them due to their desire to feed. Whatever the case, it was apparent the small group was unarmed and backed against a burning building. If someone didn't do something to help, they were as good as dead.

I placed my knife in the sheath and returned it to my pants by the small of my back. Then I grabbed a baseball bat which I always kept near the front door in case of an intruder. I threw open the door and raced down the stairs to the asphalt driveway, where I was careful not to step on the broken body of my former landlady in the bloody spot where she had fallen early that morning. I jumped high over the corpse, appearing to almost fly through the air. I may have always been scrawny, but I could run like the wind when I had to.

I ran to Mrs. Willingham's home without hesitation, where I began swinging my bat like a war hammer. The great god Thor had nothing on me that day. Wham! The club slammed into the side of the first zombie's skull, knocking its head sideways with such force as to break its neck with an audible crack. Then I brought the bat straight down on the top-front of another creature's skull, caving it in and driving bits of cranial bone deep into the corpse's brain, rendering it inanimate once again. It fell to the ground with a thud landing next to the first destroyed corpse.

A short, elderly zombie tried to grab me, but I was too fast for him, and I brought the bat down across the thing's outstretched arms. I could hear the shattering of brittle bones as the arms went limp from the elbow down. The old zombie stood for a few seconds staring, its hands dangling uselessly at the end of shattered forearms. But looking up into the thing's face, I could see it was still just as hungry and still determined to eat me. I swung the bat again, slamming it into the thing's face, driving its broken nose cartilage and facial bones up into its brain, killing it instantly.

"Three down, about ten or more to go," I thought. As terrifying as all of this should have been, I was shocked to discover I was starting to enjoy myself. It was like a real-life video game. Don't get me wrong. I understood these ugly things and what they could do to me, but they moved so slowly and clumsily. I may not have been superhero strong, but I did have some rocking moves. I also learned, to my surprise, I was getting very good at killing these walking sacks of rotting meat.

Behind me, I heard slow, heavy footfalls and saw the corpse of a tall, muscular man staggering toward me. At first, I thought it might have been the rapist from the previous night, returned from the dead, but then I recalled how his knife had penetrated the man's brain and knew he would never rise again. I ran toward the creature winding up, prepared to knock this one out of the ballpark. When I got within a foot or two, I jumped up and slammed the bat into the thing's head with such ferocity that the bat cracked, leaving me holding the jagged handle end, which was now about a foot, and a half long.

The big zombie stagger-stepped once or twice but regained its footing, coming for me again with its long arms outstretched. I pushed the jagged end of the bat into the massive creature's wide-open mouth and didn't stop shoving until it broke through the back of the thing's neck, severing its spine. I managed to step aside just in time as the colossal creature fell face-first to the ground.

I heard a commotion erupting around me and saw, to my amazement, that the five victims had decided to follow my lead by grabbing various implements lying about and fighting back. One older man had picked up the front end of my splintered bat and had driven it up through the jaw of one of the more enormous creatures and into its brain.

A young boy of about sixteen had picked up some large stones from Mrs. Willingham's garden and hurled them like baseballs at the zombies. Most of his throws did little but distract the creatures. However, one of them found its mark and cracked open the skull of one of the beasts. It staggered on its feet for a moment or two before collapsing to the ground, where it kicked and thrashed for a few seconds before lying permanently still.

An older woman picked up a discarded bottle and, like a cowboy in an old western movie, broke the bottom against the side of the brick building, leaving her with a sharp jagged weapon. Despite her age, and small size, the woman shoved the jagged business end of the bottle into the face of an approaching zombie, and although it didn't kill the creature outright, it did slow it down long enough for me to pull out my knife, and plunge it up, and into the thing's nose to it moldering brain.

Some debris had started to fall from Mrs. Willingham's burning house, and one of the men picked up a flaming piece of wood and set the clothing of an approaching woman zombie on fire. The thing stood turning in circles as if disoriented and having no idea which way to go as flames engulfed its clothing. Its flesh began to bubble, then slough off its bones along with tendons and muscle. The man left the creature standing, consumed by the fire. The monster stood for a few minutes more before it collapsed to the ground.

There were only four or five of the creatures left, and I felt confident we would be victorious. We each grabbed our makeshift weapons and waited for the remaining zombies to attack. But before the creatures got to us, the air around us erupted with the sound of gunfire. One by one, the horrid undead beasts' heads exploded in a shower of brains and blood. Within a few seconds, all of the zombies lay motionless on the ground.

"What the hell just happened?" One of the survivors said.

"We just saved your hides from that cluster of hungry zombies," a voice said from somewhere out in the street, "That's what just happened."

CHAPTER 7

A man walked toward us, stepping over the corpses as he did. He stepped on one of the corpses' outstretched hands several times, accidentally or otherwise, producing the sickening crackling sound of bones breaking. Nonchalantly, he kicked aside a splattered skull along the way, never appearing to notice. I suddenly got a very uncomfortable feeling about this character.

"My name is Captain Nathan P. Stokes," he said by way of introduction, "And these fine men are members of my newly formed anti-zombie militia. We don't have an official name as of yet, but one will be forthcoming."

Stokes wore a makeshift uniform consisting of black motorcycle boots, dark jeans, a black tee-shirt, and a black trucker's cap. There were no logos or emblems anywhere on his outfit, although I assumed that when his militia found their name sometime in the future, both the shirt and hat would have one. He was a well-built man in his late thirties with a thick mustache straight out of a twentieth-century porno flick and the steady, piercing charismatic eyes of someone in charge.

The rest of his band of merry men slowly made their way forward. Most of the survivors looked as terrified of the militiamen as they were of the zombies. These characters looked like trouble waiting to happen. If someone were to tell me Stokes broke them out of prison, I wouldn't have been even slightly shocked. For whatever reason, I wasn't frightened, but I was being cautious and was more than a little curious. The other so-called soldiers in Stokes' group were all dressed like the way he was with a variety of home-grown paramilitary garb. They were all heavily armed with handguns, rifles, swords, knives, and other weapons.

Stokes said with an unreadable expression that made me feel very uncomfortable, "Well, now what do we have here? I couldn't help but notice quite a few of these maggot motels already dead when we arrived. Which of you were responsible for taking so many of those things down?"

I decided not to say anything, unsure what this strange band of mercenaries might have in mind. The gang could be the helpful, good guys they wanted us to believe they were, or they could be something else entirely. None of them looked like their wiring was quite up to code. Then again, the lines separating sanity from insanity had become quite blurred. I was now living in a brave new bizarre world in the making.

"That guy did," the young boy suddenly said, pointing at me. I wish he hadn't done that. I was going for a low profile here, doing my best to blend into the woodwork. The boy persisted, "We were trapped, and he just showed up as a superhero with a baseball bat and started cracking heads."

I felt I'd better say something to try to downplay things a bit, "Actually, it was all of us working together." I hoped that didn't sound as lame and filled with false humility to them as it did to me. But I didn't want to stand out to these characters. I learned in high school when the room was overflowing with narcissistic psychopaths who were bigger than you and meaner than a steaming pile of cat crap; it's always best to make yourself as invisible as possible.

"No, it wasn't so much us as it was him," another voice piped up, "He was incredible!"

The older man said, "Yeah! He just jumped into the middle of a dozen of those things without taking a second to worry about his own skin. He beat them all senseless, saving my wife and son. He did that for us, total strangers. We were just five people who didn't know him from Adam. Hell, I still don't know who he is, but as far as I'm concerned, he's a hero." He turned and looked at me with his hand outstretched, "Many thanks to you, friend. My family and I owe you more than you can know."

"Great, just great," I thought.

The leader of the ragtag militia turned to me with a curious look and said, "So you took on this horde of zombies single-handed?, and what happens to be your name, Mr. Hero."

His choice of wording was quite disturbing. He approved of what I had done, yet there was a note of distrust and perhaps jealousy in his tone. I wasn't sure if he was sarcastic or if he was sincere. Either way, I decided to continue to be careful.

I hesitated then said, "It's Del; I mean, I'm D. B. Jones."

"D.B. is it?" The man questioned, "Would you care to tell me what the D. B. stands for?"

I had no intention of saying, "Delbert Bertram," and wasn't sure what I was going to say when a voice from down the alley spoke up shouting, "It stands for Death Bringer."

Everyone turned to look down the street to see where the voice had originated. I was shocked to see the girl from the previous night, the one who had almost been raped by the lunatic I accidentally killed in the alley. Thankfully, she had gotten changed at some point in time and was now fully clothed. Yet, I thought her timing couldn't be worse. Here I was trying to blend in, and between the crowd and this girl, they were putting me up on a pedestal, one I had no interest in occupying.

"I call him Death Bringer Jones because he saved my life last night," she said, "A maniac was trying to rape and murder me a few blocks from here, and Death Bringer showed up and killed the bastard. If it weren't for him, I'd be dead now. He's a real-life superhero."

"It, it wasn't . . . I mean," I stammered, trying to downplay the encounter. I hadn't meant to kill the attacker; I didn't have either the strength or the nerve to do such a thing. If the idiot hadn't tripped over those stupid pants and fallen onto my knife, that story would have turned out very differently, and I certainly wouldn't be here to tell any tales.

"He's a real hero," the girl repeated even louder, "And a humble hero as well."

Then she walked over and kissed me on the lips again, just as she had done the previous night. But, this time, she made the kiss linger for a moment, then slid the tip of her tongue between my lips. A murmur of appreciation came from the crowd of onlookers. A moment later, she pulled away, turned to the group, raised her fist into the air, and shouted. "Long live Death Bringer Jones."

Soon she, and the crowd was all repeating a chorus of "Death Bringer Jones, Death Bringer Jones, Death Bringer Jones." The girl and the survivors turned and began walking away, still repeating their chants. As they passed me, each shook my hand or patted me on the shoulder, thanking me for coming to their rescue.

It was all bizarre and surreal. I mean, what was that girl even doing still wandering around the streets? Didn't she have a home? You would think after what she went through, she'd be hiding out somewhere safe. Hell, that's what I had done, and what were the chances she'd show up here telling everyone that weird name she had come up with for me?

One of them, the young boy of about sixteen turned, and said as he hurried to catch the departing crowd, "My name's Jack, and it's an honor to shake your hand. You're a real hero, Death Bringer. I'll never forget what you did for us today." He seemed to be studying my face as he spoke.

I didn't bother to correct him, nor did I try to explain how my actions had nothing to do with heroism because I knew it would be pointless. Instead, I remained silent and nodded, acknowledging the compliment. Little did I realize at the time, that young boy was an amateur illustrator. Eventually, he would create the exaggerated cartoon superhero version of Death Bringer Jones. That cartoon would be greatly responsible not only for my fame but for the direction my life would eventually take.

After the crowd had made their way down the street, with the cries of "Death Bringer Jones" fading in the distance, Captain Stokes turned to me and said, "Death Bringer? Humm . . . yeah, I like that. Death Bringer. It just slides right off your tongue. Don't you agree, boys?" A series of low grunts of agreement flowed from the frightening-looking group of muscle-bound mercenaries. Stokes asked, "So Death Bringer, are you looking for a job?"

"A job?" I asked, surprised. "No. I have a job, or I should say I did have a job. But now that I think about it, maybe not anymore. I suppose there's little call for a customer service representative with zombies taking over the world."

"Right, you are DB. Can I call you DB?" He suddenly went into what I considered his sales pitch, not waiting for my reply, "Good, DB it is. You see, DB, people like you and I are destined for greater things in a world such as this one. The old ways, our old jobs are gone now. We have to find new opportunities to make money. We can't wait for the opportunities to come to us; we have to make our destiny, and guess what? The job most in demand as of twenty-four hours ago just became zombie killers. Welcome to your new profession, Death Bringer Jones, zombie slayer."

I thought all of this sounded much better than it might be. Yes, I may have survived so far, but as I said, a lot of that was pure luck. The funny thing about luck was you couldn't count on it; it could change in a heartbeat. I didn't consider myself either brave or daring. Then again, I did attack a bunch of zombies to help those people. But now that I thought about it, that wasn't heroic. It was just plain stupid. I suspected if I went with these guys, I might find myself dead before too long. Looking at the condition of this motley group, I wasn't sure I was any safer from them than I was from the undead. I decided to ask a few questions.

"So, who's going to pay for this zombie-killing service anyway? And what good is money if the world is in ruins?"

"As far as who will pay, at first, it will be individuals or perhaps clusters of survivors who want to be free from worrying about being attacked by the creatures. You know, perhaps wealthy neighborhoods or maybe small towns. But eventually, I think the government will get involved in some way, either local governments or even national," Stokes replied.

"But look around you," I argued, "Look at this town burning, with no electric power, not enough firefighters or police. It's chaos. How long do you think it will be until there's no more government?"

Stokes seemed to think about that for a moment, then said, "You may be right about the governments, at least in the short term. The world may sink into anarchy for a short time, but as the saying goes, this too will pass. In the meantime, it will be up to people like us, me, and my boys here, and hopefully, you, Death Bringer, to do what we can to maintain control."

I noticed his interesting choice of words. I had a feeling this was more about control for Stokes than anything; I asked, "And what if the people you help have no money or nothing of value?"

Stokes hesitated again for a beat or two, then said, "Everyone has something of value, whether its cash, jewelry, or perhaps personal services if you know what I mean." He gave a sly smile that I didn't like very much. I recalled seeing that same look on the rapist's face the previous night.

"I'll have to give it some thought," I said non committally. I suddenly wanted to be anywhere but standing in the street alone encircled by this band of potential maniacs.

"Well, while you're giving it some thought, let me introduce you to a few of my merry men."

Stokes signaled to a large muscular man who appeared to be in his mid-thirties, although it was difficult to determine his age. His dull black eyes sat deep under thick brows, and his nose was broad. His face appeared to have been chiseled out of granite. I wouldn't have been shocked if that face was equally as hard as a stone.

The man wore a yellowed blood-stained wife-beater tee shirt tucked into black cargo pants with numerous pockets. He had several pistols and knives strategically located around his body hanging from belts and holsters. He wore black leather motorcycle boots, and I suspected there might be knives tucked down into those as well.

Stokes said, "This is Mountain, DB. He's the biggest and strongest of the group, as I'm sure you can see. He's a walking arsenal, but he doesn't need more than his fists to take down any man, living or dead."

Then Stokes pointed to another of his men, an average-sized man dressed in a black tee-shirt and matching pants. He didn't carry any guns, but he did have two long curved swords in sheaths around his belt, one on each side. The man was lean, trim, and muscular but not in a bulky way. He seemed to move with a sort of grace that the man known as Mountain didn't have.

"This is Razor. He's a fifth-degree black belt in Tai Kwon Do and a third-degree black belt in Goguru karate. His expertise, in addition to hand-to-hand combat, is the use of the double katana blades. Had we not bothered to blow those thing's heads off, Razor here would have been more than happy to remove those heads for us."

Then Stokes introduced another of his men. This guy wasn't as big as any of the others, but he had a definite look about him. It was a look I didn't like very much. The man was only about five feet eight inches tall and maybe one hundred and fifty pounds. He wore clean tight blue jeans, a black long-sleeved western-cut shirt unbuttoned at the top, re-vealing some sort of metallic chain. His belt had a sizeable gaudy buckle formed in the shape of a skull. His hair was thick, black, and combed severely back from his forehead. His complexion was weathered, tanned, and creased.

I was sure the man was older than he was trying to appear, maybe in his late forties. I also sensed by the way he held himself that he was muscular as well as strong. He had what I thought of as a tough and rugged swagger about him. The fact was, he looked just plain dangerous.

The most disturbing features about the man were his strange smile and his penetrating eyes. I didn't quite know how to explain it, but I felt the two facial expressions seemed to contradict each other. His clean-shaven face and pleasant smile alone appeared friendly enough, although a bit forced. But his eyes bore a look unlike anything I had ever seen before. I was sure that was the look of complete insanity.

I thought to myself, "He's trying his best to look like a normal person, but he's not fooling anybody." He seemed to be both alive and dead at the same time. Maybe it was my imagination running away with me, or perhaps I had just read one too many graphic novels. Regardless, there was no way that man standing there was anything but bad.

Stokes said, "This is Stanley Shabowsky. However, he prefers to go by the name Deimos. It's something an associate of his from down in Yuengsville came up with, or so I'm told. Whatever the case, I go along with it because he likes it, and I like him. It has a nice, frightening ring to it. Deimos is someone I keep around for special projects requiring his unique skill set."

I wondered with dread what that unique skill set might be. There was something about this Deimos character that sent involuntary chills racing down my spine. Maybe it was the cold, dead look of those probing eyes. More likely, it was the madness that seemed to lurk just under the surface.

I was suddenly feeling a bit uncertain about Deimos and Stokes and the rest of his group. Nevertheless, I had to give Stokes credit for how quickly he took advantage of a horrible situation and found a way to turn it into a money-making proposition. The crisis was less than twenty-four hours old, and he had already formed a mini-army of mercenaries with a plan to profit from slaughtering zombies. No one could say he wasn't an opportunist. But it was apparent these men had been together for some time. This zombie thing may have been their latest scam, but they undoubtedly had been involved in criminal activities before.

Stokes went around introducing the remaining members of his team, and I couldn't help but feel intimidated by the giant, angry-looking muscle-bound warriors. Yet, no matter how huge or how frightening, none of them bothered me as much as that creepy Deimos weirdo. He reminded me of someone who might sneak up on you, slit your throat in your sleep, and smile the whole time he was doing it.

"Look, DB," Stokes said, "I know you probably think you're not as tough as these guys, but you have something I need. You're fast, agile, and fearless from what those people have said, and that's every bit as important to me as brute strength. So don't sweat it. We can work on building you up and making you look scarier. I realize that image crap doesn't mean anything to zombies, but the public eats that sort of thing up, and satisfying the public translates to financial opportunity. With the right public relations, we can make Death Bringer Jones a household name. Then we can trade on that reputation to bring in the bucks."

I said, "Look, Captain Stokes, I truly appreciate your most generous offer, but honestly, I don't think I'm ready to be part of your crew right now, no matter what you might believe about me. I'm honored by your consideration, but I think I need to go it alone for a while until I figure out where I belong in this strange new world."

Stokes hesitated then said, "I respect your honesty, DB, but you have to admit, there is safety in numbers. This zombie killing isn't the sort of thing you should try on your own, my friend. Besides, you have as much to fear from the living as the dead."

"Yeah. I learned that firsthand," I agreed, not knowing whether I should take the man's comment as a threat. I noticed Deimos staring a hole through me. He still wore that strange half-smile, reminding me of a lion looking at a gazelle. I had a feeling if Stokes ordered him to jump on me and rip my throat out with his teeth, he wouldn't hesitate.

I said, "I need some time to sort a few things out first. Maybe later, a few days or weeks from now. I don't know."

"In a few weeks, DB, you, me, and every living creature in this country could be dead, or should I say undead?" There are no guarantees for any of us anymore."

"Understood," I said, then I turned to head back to my apartment, and I said, "Thanks for everything, Captain. I truly do appreciate it."

I wasn't sure how the mercenaries would react to my refusal. I might have been about to get a bullet in the back of my skull. Or perhaps I might become one of those special projects the Captain saved for Deimos. I suspected not only would he be eager to do it, but he would enjoy it as well. But to my pleasure, my violent death never came.

"Then I suppose we'll see you when we see you," Stokes replied, "Stay strong, and stay well, Death Bringer Jones." I didn't turn around. I didn't care if I ever looked into Deimos's dead eyes again. I knew I would never forget his creepy name either.

Then as quickly as they had arrived, the group of mercenaries was gone. I slowly made my way back to my apartment, not knowing what the future would hold for me.

CHAPTER 8

For the next week or so, I didn't leave my apartment. I mean, I did occasionally sneak out to dump my plastic bucket, turned chamber pot as well as dirty wash water. But other than that, I stayed inside. I was waiting, for what exactly? I wasn't sure, but I knew all that awaited me outside was trouble. Some might think it was an act of cowardice, and in a way, maybe it was, but I preferred to think of it as simply being precautious. The world outside was changing rapidly, and not for the better.

Occasionally during the day, I would look out my front window, down at the street below, but it always seemed to be abandoned. I figured any regular, law-abiding citizens were doing the same as me, laying low and hiding out. I had seen a sampling of what the world was becoming with zombies, looters, and rapists wandering the streets. In addition, now there were bands of wannabe mercenaries out there trying to make a buck from a horrible situation. I decided I simply didn't want to be part of any of it. So, I continued to hide out in my apartment.

I knew sooner or later I was going to run out of cereal, chips, pretzels, beef sticks, and crackers, but for now, I was doing ok. I was, however, going to have to go out soon and find some water. The containers I had filled on the first day were running low, and I only had a few bottles of brand-named water left. Like it or not, I'd have to suck it up and go out there among who knows what.

As I said before, I had always idolized the many superheroes in my various graphic novels, and I liked to think of myself as being every bit as noble as those characters. I think that was why I had gotten such a bad vibe from Captain Stokes' group and why I had turned them down.

I truly wanted to help. I needed to make a difference. I wanted to matter, and a part of me even wanted the world to know and respect my name. But I didn't believe being part of some paramilitary group would do anything to help me attain those goals. Besides, something felt wrong with that group. I couldn't put my finger on what that might be, but something just seemed out of place. This feeling was especially true of that Deimos character. Something was off with him. I was glad I walked away from their offer. Hell, I was delighted I survived walking away from their offer.

I had also been lucky that the fires, which had so decimated Franksville, had not made it back to my detached garage apartment. For a while, it was like the madness encompassing the world had chosen to ignore me completely. But as is always true, all good things must come to an end. One afternoon I noticed my last bottle of water had run dry. As I was relaxing in my recliner, reading a book by the limited sunlight light shining in through the living room window, I heard the thunder of what sounded like dozens of footfalls in a synchronized march coming from outside. Then I heard trucks rumbling down the street right outside my apartment.

There came a booming voice of what sounded like a pre-recorded message coming over some sort of loudspeaker or public address system. The announcement repeated in a continuous loop. It said, "Attention all living citizens over the age of eighteen. You are required by a direct order from the President of the United States to leave your homes immediately and report to the unit commander of the division of the US Army currently assigned to this town. Failure to report for conscription will be considered an act of treason and will be handled accordingly. Punishment for such an offense will be death."

My breath caught in my throat as I looked out the window and saw several dozen armed, uniformed men going from door to door in those buildings, which were still standing, and coming out with men and women of all ages. I realized I had no choice but to go down and see what was going on. I knew what conscription meant; it was the draft. I found it ironic how the same military that had rejected me no more than a few months earlier was now rounding up anyone with a pulse and putting them into this man's army.

I put on a pair of black motorcycle boots, hiding my snakeskins in the closet, and black jeans with a plain black tee shirt. I tucked my hunting knife in its sheath back into my pants, and after covering it with my shirttail. I locked the front door as I left—more out of habit than anything -, and headed down the stairs.

"Sir, please follow me," a voice came from my left as I reached the bottom of the stairway.

"Excuse me?" I asked as I turned and looked into the eyes of a young man not much older than I was, dressed in an army uniform holding an automatic rifle at the ready. "What did you say?"

"I said, Sir, will you please come with me?"

"And if I said no thanks?" I asked, feeling confident I already knew the answer.

The young man's face took on a more serious and stern expression, and he replied as he pointed the gun directly at my face, "I'm afraid I'll have to insist, Sir."

Forceful but polite, I thought. Indeed, it sounded like the military to me.

"Well then. In that case, lead on, my friend," I said as he directed me to walk down the street toward a small crowd of people gathering around several large military trucks. I suppose some of them were neighbors of mine, although I couldn't be sure since I didn't know any of my neighbors. These folks were likely hiding in their homes, just like I had been.

Maybe a few of the others had followed the convoy from nearby neighborhoods. Some were likely part of the group, perhaps recently drafted, as they didn't have uniforms. I suspected they congregated in my area since it was the least affected by the fires, and being at the edge of town had more open spaces for a meeting.

When we reached the group of several dozen men and women of various ages, a middle-aged man in a crisp army uniform made his way up atop one of the flatbed trucks. He stood straight, and tall not saying a word, hands folded behind his back, looking out over the crowd, waiting patiently for the talking to stop, which it eventually did. When there was complete silence, he spoke.

"Ladies and gentlemen. My name is Colonel James Deacon of the United States Army. As you have noticed, we have something of a crisis on our hands, which has developed not just in your fine town or in our great country, but worldwide. The dead are indeed rising and feeding on the living. The reason for this anomaly remains unknown at this time. However, from all indications, it appears a virus of some sort may have caused this. As best as we can determine, those living are unaffected.

"The virus activates only upon the death of its host. If the problem is viral, we must assume that every living human was affected and carries the virus. We assume this is why after death, the host body revives to become a walking corpse. We have not yet figured out why this occurs, nor do we understand why this revived cadaver has a craving for living human flesh. However, this nonetheless is the situation. From all indications, the only way to destroy these creatures is to either destroy their brains or separate their heads from their bodies. Setting them ablaze also does a good job of eradicating them, although it is less effective and time-consuming. Now you may wonder why we have asked you all here."

"Asked? No one asked me! I was brought here by force!" A voice shouted from the crowd.

"Yeah. Me too!" Another yelled, followed by several more. Soon numerous complaints and arguments were coming from the unwilling gathering.

Once again, Colonel Deacon was silent, staring hard at the crowd waiting for the voices to go quiet. After a few moments, he nodded his head at a nearby soldier, who raised his rifle into the air, and fired off an ear-reverberating round.

The crowd went silent, and he continued, "We are in crisis mode, people. The armies of the dead are rapidly increasing in number. Very soon, they will overtake those of us who remain alive. In addition, there are clusters of living humans who have participated in the most heinous crimes such as rape, murder, looting, and vandalism. At present, most law-abiding citizens have as much to fear from the living as the dead. The government has instituted drastic countermeasures to maintain civilization as we know it. So, like it or not, people, we are at war. This war is not in some foreign country where you can learn about it on the evening news. This war is right here on our sovereign American soil."

"So why doesn't the army take care of them? Isn't that why we pay taxes?" A voice shouted.

"Yeah!" Others shouted. "Yeah!"

For a third time, the Colonel waited patiently for the crowd to grow silent. This time they did so without the need for a warning shot. The Colonel said, "The fine men and women of our armed forces are doing what they can to fight to win back our precious freedom and our way of life. But unfortunately, we are too few. However, we are taking steps to remedy that situation. We now come to the reason why you all are here."

The people in the crowd began to look at each other questioningly as low murmurs began circulating among them.

Colonel Deacon smiled knowingly and said, "Congratulations are in order, ladies and gentlemen. From this moment on, all of you can consider yourselves soldiers in the United States Army. You will be responsible for assisting in the war against the undead. Welcome one and all."

"What?" A young man shouted, "You can't do that! You can't force us to be part of this if we don't want to."

"Not only can we do this, Sir, but we have," Colonel Deacon said sternly. "And as a soldier in the US Army, failure to comply with a direct order from the Commander, and Chief of said armed forces, that person being the President of the United States of America, will be considered an act of treason. Also, failure to comply with the rules and regulations of this man's army will be considered insubordination in the extreme. Either of these acts during a time of war in the field of battle is punishable by death. And for the record, you are now standing on the field of battle."

"Screw you, G.I. Joe!" A man of about thirty shouted, "This is America, dammit, and no one can tell me what I can and can't do. It's a free country, and I spit on your rules, your orders, and your precious Commander in Chief. Hell, I didn't even vote for that Bozo."

The man started to walk away. As he did, others turned as if they, too, were considering leaving. I stood perfectly still, watching with great interest, not sure what might happen next. But I had read enough books and seen enough movies to suspect what would occur. If I was right, things were about to get real nasty, real fast. Colonel Deacon nodded to one of his troops on the ground, and the man raised his rifle, pointing it directly at the departing man, who was heading his way. The man stopped in his track.

The man turned and angrily shouted at the Colonel, repeating, "You can't do this. This is America, dammit!"

"Please stop, Sir, and you won't be harmed," the soldier said from behind his rifle. But the man wouldn't listen and kept walking away. The soldier looked toward the Colonel on his truck. The commander gave an almost imperceptible nod to his subordinate. A moment later, a shot rang out, and the man's head exploded in a shower of brains, bone, and blood. His lifeless and practically headless body dropped to the ground.

The crowd went dead silent. As my late grandpa would have said, "The only sound was dozens of assholes slamming shut."

Then I could hear crying coming from some people in the crowd. The Colonel looked over the masses at first without saying a word. Then he let out a sigh of apparent regret and said, "I'm sorry, people. That was very unfortunate. However, it was necessary. Now, I trust there won't be any more deserters among you fine recruits."

There wasn't as much as a single protest from anyone in the group. One man did have to help hold up a young woman who had turned pale and looked as if she might pass out. I suddenly had what seemed like a thousand questions going through my mind all at once. But all I could think to do was stand silently and await my orders from, who? My commander? Had I just been drafted into the army? Were these people army personnel? Or could they be more of those mercenary militia types posing as an army? Could they force me to be part of this? Of course, they could. I had just witnessed what happened to anyone who refused.

"You there, recruit," I heard a voice say. I looked up and saw the Colonel staring right at me.

"Me?" I asked. "Are you talking to me?"

"It's SIR!" The Colonel shouted, "Are you talking to me, SIR!"

"Um, sorry. I mean, sorry, SIR!"

"Very good, recruit. What's your name, soldier?"

I hesitated for a moment. I correctly assumed this wasn't a very good time to bring up the whole "Death Bringer" thing. I said, "D . . . Delbert, Delbert Jones, Sir."

"Excellent, Private Jones. Now here's what I want you to do, and this goes for everyone." He was now addressing the gathering, "Each of you will return home, accompanied by one of my soldiers. You will get whatever minimal provisions my people instruct you to pack, along with appropriate clothing. Unfortunately, because of the current situation, we won't have uniforms for most of you, and we'll have to gather weapons as we can from wherever we can. If you have weapons of your own, please show them to your escorts for approval. The important thing to remember is that you come to the battle prepared to fight. We have to take back your town and our country from these undead mindless bastards. And don't you get any ideas about fragging any of my people either. Such actions will be dealt with quickly and permanently. It's now 11:42 hours. Be back here and ready to move out by 12:30 hours."

A moment later, a young female soldier approached me and said, "Private Jones. I'm Sergeant Samantha Cruz, and I will be escorting you back to get your supplies. I must remind you that you are a conscript of the US Army, and any attempts to flee will be an act of treason, and I will treat such an act with severe retaliation. Do I make myself clear?"

Sergeant Cruz was an attractive young woman about my age. She had short black hair hidden under her military cap and large dark eyes. In my opinion, usually, women in military garb can do very little to make themselves look attractive, which I suppose is how it's supposed to be. Still, this Samantha Cruz was the exception to that rule. I suspected she'd even look good dressed in a burlap potato sack.

"Um, yeah," I said, "I mean yes Sir, or yes Ma'am or whatever I'm supposed to say. You don't have to worry; I won't run. I tried to enlist in the army a while back. It's something I've always wanted."

"Very good," she snapped angrily, "Then how about you stop flapping your gums and rambling on about your unimportant life story, and we'll be on our way. We don't have a lot of time."

I said, "Sure. No problem. I mean, yes, Ma'am. I just live over there in an apartment above that garage, Ma'am."

A few minutes later, we were both in my apartment. Sergeant Cruz was standing near the open front door as I gathered a few pairs of pants, a couple of tee shirts, some socks, and underwear from my dresser. I stuffed them into a backpack along with a tube of toothpaste, some deodorant, and an unopened bar of soap. Then I went to my closet to grab a jacket.

"If you have a rifle or pistol in there, you are encouraged to bring them along, but I would suggest telling me about it first, so I don't get nervous and blow your damn fool head off," Cruz said.

"Yes, Ma'am. I don't have a gun, Ma'am. I could never afford one," I told her, "But now I wish I did have one."

I had made sure my tee-shirt was long enough to hide the knife, which I tucked into my pants, and as far as I could tell, this Cruz woman hadn't realized I had it. I walked closer to her noticing she had relaxed her hold on her rifle, having determined I wasn't any threat. When I got within a foot of her, I carefully reached around my back with one hand while grabbing her arm and pulling her off balance with the other. Within a second, I had my knife pressed tightly to her throat.

"Drop the rifle, and do it now," I demanded.

"You're making a big mistake, mister," she said as she let her rifle drop to the floor, "When the Colonel learns about this, you'll be a dead man for sure."

I said in as stern a voice as I could come up with, "Don't move and don't speak unless you're answering my questions. Is that clear?"

"Ok. I got that. Now ask away, tough guy." I could tell she wasn't in the least bit frightened by me but was being cautious, nonetheless.

I said, "Ok, here's what I need to know, and this is critical. If you lie to me, I think I'll know it. Are you and those others out there truly members of the United States Army? Or are you just another band of mercenaries out to earn a buck off a horrible situation?"

"Would that matter to you?"

"Yes. That would matter very much. I was recently asked to join such a group, and I turned them down. I'm not interested. If this truly is the army, then I would be honored to be a member. So, what is it, Sergeant?"

She hesitated for a moment, then said, "First of all, yes, we are a legitimate division of the US Army, and we are most definitely not mercenaries or outlaws. Secondly, we would be glad to have men with strong convictions like yours as part of the US Army, and third, if you don't take that knife away from my throat, you're going to find your balls scattered all around this room."

I felt a bump against the front of my pants and carefully looked down. I saw that somehow, and I had no idea how; she had managed to get a pistol from somewhere, and it was now pointed directly at my crotch. I quickly pulled the knife away from her throat and carefully backed away with my arms raised and a look of embarrassment on my face.

CHAPTER 9

After that humiliating encounter with the lovely Ms. Cruz, I dejectedly followed her back to the area where everyone had congregated initially as Colonel Deacon has ordered. The Colonel was still on the back of the flatbed with his arms clasped behind his back.

Once the crowd became quiet, he said, "If I may repeat myself, ladies, and gentlemen, welcome to the United States Army. We thank you in advance for your service. You may be wondering what your first assignment will be. Well, wonder no more ladies and gentlemen. Beginning immediately, we will assume the task of ridding this fine community of all undead beings. Our goal is two-fold. First, we will eradicate all of the zombies. Secondly, we will construct a barrier around this town to prevent any other undead from getting inside.

"Similar activities will be taking place simultaneously in many towns and cities around the country. Even though this town isn't a big one, we'll have our work cut out for us people. I can't begin to tell you when we'll have electricity and running water once again. It's far too early in the war for that, and make no mistake about it, people, we are at war. So first we must clean up this town. Remember, people, the only way to bring these things down is to either kill the brain, sever the spinal column, or decapitate the head. So, no matter how scared you might be, we will win the day if you don't panic and remember what I've told you.

"I apologize for your having to go into battle untrained, but the situation is a dire one. As such, I must warn you, some of you may fall in combat. That's a simple fact of war. If one of your fellow soldiers should die, they will become one of those creatures within minutes, perhaps seconds. If that should happen, you must put aside your emotions and no longer think of this creature as who it once was. Instead, you must know it for the hideous monster it has become. I repeat, do not hesitate to out down these creatures, former friends or not. Now let's go out there, people, and destroy these walking puss-sacks."

Then Cruz and several other uniformed soldiers began dividing the recruits into small squads. Cruz signaled for me to join her group. I didn't get the impression she had done this out of any respect for me or desire to have me on her team. I believed it was more likely that she didn't completely trust me after our encounter in the apartment and wanted to keep me within controlling distance.

Along with Cruz and me, there were three other squad members. One was an average height stocky man of about fifty who wore blue jeans, a red-checkered flannel shirt, a black ball cap, and work boots. He didn't have a gun but carried a four-foot length of galvanized pipe, which looked like a weapon specifically designed to use on the types of monsters we would encounter. He had a severe you-don't-screw-with-me look about him that must have come from a lifetime of brawling experience.

The second recruit looked as if he was the exact opposite of the first. He was tall, nerdy, and thinner than me. Even though he carried a sword, he didn't look in any way threatening. When I looked closer, his sword had ornate carvings on the handle and a variety of detailed etchings along the blade. It was either a prop blade or one of those low-cost nerd swords you could buy online. Chances were it would likely break in half the first time the guy tried to use it. He looked like the proverbial deer in the headlights. I could tell it was very likely that this guy was lunch in our first encounter with any zombies. He was as dead as the creatures we were hunting. He just didn't know it yet.

The third new member of our team was a woman of about thirty-five. She was well-built with an athletic body, close-cropped dark hair, and a no-nonsense bulldog look about her. Although she seemed as uncertain about what was happening as the rest of us, I got the impression she would quickly adapt and do just fine when things got rough. I was right about that.

Cruz said, "Alright, everyone, here's the plan. Starting over there on Arch Street, we're going to go door-to-door and look for deadheads. Got it?"

Everyone nodded in agreement, and Cruz shouted, "Don't stand there nodding your damn fool heads like some sort of bobblehead dolls. Whenever a superior officer asks you a question, you will respond with yes, Ma'am. Do I make myself clear?"

"Yes, Ma'am," I responded, with a bit more enthusiasm than I should have. Cruz looked at me like I was trying to be a smartass or something, which, to be completely honest, I was. I suspected I might have pushed her wrong buttons, and she was about to make an example of me when fortunately for me, someone else on the team shouted, "Yes, Sir!"

Thank goodness. Someone else had said something even dumber. I could tell this wasn't going to end well. Cruz's eyes held a death stare, which I followed in a direction leading straight to the tall, skinny guy with the nerd sword. It looked to me like he might not have to wait for a bunch of dead ones to take him out; he was doing an excellent job on his own. Cruz walked right up to the guy, who was supposed to be standing at attention but slouched pitifully. He stood up straighter when Cruz approached him, but instead of focusing eyes front, he was looking right at her. Seriously? I mean, any idiot who's ever seen an army movie knows you don't eyeball your commanding officer.

Granted, my over-the-top reply of "Yes Ma'am" might have skirted the line a bit, but this guy not only crossed it but now he was about to trip over it and fall face-first into a steaming roadside cow pie.

"What is your name, soldier?" Cruz shouted from just inches from his face.

"Huh?" The idiot replied.

"Wrong answer," I thought to myself; this was going to be good.

"Did you just say 'huh' to me, maggot? Would you please tell me I was mistaken? I'll tell you what, chump. Let's give this one another try. Recruit what is your name?"

He hesitated for a moment as if contemplating the answer to some mystery of the ages. Then after a bit, he said, "Peter. Peter Schultz."

"Peter Schultz what?" Cruz shouted, expecting to hear Ma'am somewhere in his reply.

"Just Peter Shultz. That all. Unless you want my middle name, which is Benjamin."

"Tell me Private Peter, Benjamin Shultz. Did your momma have any kids that lived? Because as best as I can tell, you're every bit as brain dead as one of those walking meat-sacks out there. Is that true Private?, and let me warn you if your answer doesn't end with 'Ma'am,' you're gonna curse your momma forever bringing you into this world."

Shultz hesitated for a long moment, then said, "Sorry. I forgot the question, Ma'am."

"Never mind, Private; you just answered my question for me."

Cruz looked at me and gave me a brief knowing smile. I could tell she was as confident as I was about Peter Shultz's minimal chance for survival in this strange new world. She looked across the street and pointed at a home, which appeared to be well intact.

"That's our first assignment, people. We're going to make sure that place is zombie-free, and if it isn't, then we're going to clear it. Once we have completed our mission, we're going to lock it up and mark it cleared. Now let's do this thing, people. Private Shultz, you're on point."

"Point, Ma'am? I don't understand what that means, Ma'am," Shultz said with genuine confusion.

"What it means, soldier, is you will take the lead, and we will follow. Not to worry, Private, we have your six."

The only thought, which came to mind for me was "cannon fodder."

CHAPTER 10

The first group of homes was a collection of six two-story wood-framed row houses. We started with the house on the far-left end with plans to hit each one until they were all cleared. Schultz approached the front door cautiously, obviously worried about what he might find inside. He stood staring at the door with his ridiculously goofy warrior sword gripped tightly in his right hand and his left hand reaching out cautiously for the knob as if he had somehow forgotten how to open a door.

Suddenly, a large boot flew up alongside Shultz, striking the door hard; Cruz's foot splintered the doorjamb and threw the door open.

"Jesus H. Rodriguez, Shultz!" Cruz shouted, "What are you waiting for, a personal invitation?"

With that, she pushed Shultz into the house. We followed in his stumbling wake.

Cruz shouted, "Fan out and check every room, every closet, the basement, and even under every bed. Once you clear a room, shout 'clear' and then move on to the next room. If you encounter any of those walking beef sticks people, do not hesitate to destroy them immediately. And remember people, you have to kill the head to kill them, dead."

I wondered where she picked up that catchy little slogan. I decided I'd tuck that one away for future reference. Since I was going to build a new career in the army killing zombies, I figured I might as well collect all the knowledge I could. I thought of these tiny pearls of wisdom as Zombie Slayer Rules and decided to record them as they might come in handy down the road. This one would be Zombie slayer Rule #1: Kill the head to kill them, dead.

Suddenly I heard a gut-wrenching scream and saw Shultz falling backward and landing on the floor just a few feet in front of me. He was writhing and holding his hand on his throat as a fountain of blood spurted out between his fingers. Earlier I had figured him for nothing more than cannon fodder. I had hoped I would be wrong about that, but unfortunately, I wasn't.

Coming out of a nearby room and lurching toward us was an older man I vaguely recognized. In life, he may have been someone I had seen around town at one time or another. But in death, with his snapping mouth filled with the blood and torn flesh of the recently deceased Private Peter Benjamin Schultz, I wasn't sure. Either way, it was clear the thing's appetite had not been satisfied, and it thought I should serve as its next main course.

I suddenly realized the only weapon I had available was my knife, and the idea of getting it stuck in another zombie skull still rubbed me the wrong way. That was when I noticed Shultz's novelty sword sticking out of the approaching creature's stomach. The dead private either didn't pay attention to Cruz's slogan, or he panicked. As the beast shambled forward, I grabbed the handle of the sword, put my foot against his stomach, pushed while ripping it from the dead thing's guts, simultaneously tearing a large opening and spilling its innards onto the floor with a sickening plopping sound.

The monster stood for a moment, uncertain of what had just happened. It was looking down at its leaking innards. I took advantage of its momentary distraction. I shoved the tip of the blade up through the bottom of the beast's chin. The sharp end traveled up through its pallet and into its brain. I let go of the handle as the monster collapsed in a heap to the floor. To my surprise, the blade didn't break. It was stronger than I had thought.

Unknown to me, during the few moments it took for me to kill the creature, the late Private Shultz had become one of the things himself. He was struggling to his feet, intent on chewing into the back of my unsuspecting neck.

I heard a loud whacking sound behind me and turned around to see one of my fellow recruits, that buff woman, standing with a Louisville slugger in her hands. Blood and bits of flesh and hair covered the end of the bat. The Shultz zombie lay on the ground with its head at a ninety-degree angle its body. It wasn't moving.

"Thanks," I said. "You just saved my life."

"Forget it," she replied gruffly, having already lost interest in dead Shultz and me. "We got work to do. Come on."

I walked alongside her as we made our way upstairs. "Listen, I'm D. B. Jones. What's your name?"

She looked at me with her patented tough chick look and said, "The name's Hargrove, but you can call me Ace, and in case you're getting any ideas, forget it. I pitch for the other team if you get my drift."

"Other team?" I wondered to myself. Then I realized what she meant. "Oh no, nothing like that. I'm just thankful you saved my life, is all."

She said, "I told you to forget that. Now focus on what we're doing so I don't have to save your fool ass again. You can start with that maggot condo at the top of the stairs."

I looked up and was stunned to see an older woman standing on the second-floor landing. She wore floral pajamas with a solid pink terry cloth bathrobe hanging askew from her shoulders. She or I should say, it was standing as if unsure how to navigate the stairs. The thing was staring down at me with its toothless mouth opening and closing in apparent anticipation.

That moment of uncertainty gave me time to figure out my plan of attack. I reached behind me and withdrew the blade from its sheath. I planned to race up the remaining steps and sink the thing right into its gaping gum-filled mouth and up into its brain.

As I made my final run, I heard an ear-shattering bang and saw the creature's head explode, disappearing from its shoulders. Its headless corpse stood for a second before collapsing in a heap. It fell forward and slid down a few steps before coming to a stop. Cruz walked up and grabbed the thing by the bathrobe, dragging it the rest of the way down the stairs and dropping it on top of Shultz's remains.

"Let's go, people. Let's stop fartin' around. This is serious business, as you've seen by the untimely demise of your fellow recruit Private Shultz. There's no time for wasting time. Let's kill these walking nightmares, and then go kill some more."

"Yes, Ma'am," my comrades and I all said in unison. I realized Cruze had just used another expression I'd probably steal for another day. Zombie slayer Rule #2: "There's no time for wasting time." Where did she manage to come up with these? She didn't strike me as the creative, clever sayings type. Maybe she got them from Colonel Deacon. Or perhaps she just picked them up along the way. I was going to have to write them down soon, so I didn't forget them.

Within the next ten minutes, we had cleared the house, and by the end of an hour, the entire cluster of homes was zombie-free. Fortunately, none of the homes had caught fire, or the whole block would have likely gone up. As we stopped for a brief rest, I saw several other groups working to put out fires that still burned in a nearby neighborhood.

After a few minutes, a long flatbed truck pulled up with large roles of heavy wire fencing on board. I saw Colonel Deacon walking toward us with two other small squads of recruits.

"Squad leaders!"

"Sir, yes, Sir!" All the recruits shouted as one, including Cruz.

"I want you to have your people take this fencing off the truck and stretch it tightly between these buildings being sure to secure it completely to the structures. Make sure the fence is tight, strong, and above all else, secure. Once you've done that, I'll personally examine the fencing for integrity, and may God help you it had better meet my standards."

"Sir, yes, Sir!" They all called again. For the next hour or so, we all worked together to erect a ten-foot-tall section of security fencing, which spanned an area about thirty feet wide between the cluster of homes we cleared and another house. As we worked, I saw several other recruits carrying salvaged lumber inside the buildings. I heard a lot of hammering and realized they were boarding up the outside window, essentially turning the buildings into barricades as well.

After a while, the Colonel returned and instructed us to use axes and knives to sharpen points onto the ends of various salvaged wood pieces, creating long spear-like spikes. We forced the sharp ends of the spikes through the fence at strategic locations and buried the blunt ends in the ground. By the time we had finished, we had a thirty-foot-long wall of deadly spikes jutting through the fence. To say we were exhausted was an understatement.

"Alright, people." The Colonel said. "That will be sufficient for today. I need you all well rested for first thing tomorrow morning. Your squad leaders will show you where to wash up, get some grub, and where you'll bunk for the night."

"Bunk for the night?" I thought. My apartment was only a block away. I could practically see it from where we stood.

Cruz must have guessed what I was thinking because she approached me and said, "Forget it, Jones. You are part of a squad now, and you sleep where Uncle Sam tells you to sleep. You'll eat, sleep, drink, and crap when we tell you. Is that clear, Private Jones?"

"Yes, Ma'am. Crystal clear, Ma'am," I replied, trying to sound enthusiastic although I was feeling anything but sincere.

"Outstanding, Private Jones, and are you feeling tired, Private Jones? You look tired to me."

I had no intention of letting her think I was anything less than Superman, so I said, "No, Ma'am. I am wide awake and ready for action Ma'am!" I have no idea why I said that. I don't think I was trying to impress Cruz. Hell, I didn't even like her, even though she was hot. Maybe I was hoping to show her I was every bit as tough as she was, and maybe more so. Whatever the case, my plan failed miserably.

"Excellent, Private Jones. Congratulations. You get the first watch."

"First watch, Ma'am?"

"Yes, Private Jones. It's now twenty-one hundred hours. We'll bunk inside this building. You can guard the door and watch for deadheads. Private Hargrove will take over at midnight followed three hours later by Private Lawson." She looked at both Ace Hargrove and the big serious guy, who I now knew to be Lawson.

"May I offer a suggestion, Ma'am?" I asked foolishly. "Since we have already cleared these buildings and know they are safe, couldn't we all just go inside, lock the front door, and sleep?"

Hargrove whispered to Lawson, "Oh boy, this is gonna be great!"

"Thank you, Private Jones, for your incredible words of wisdom. Perhaps you can explain to us all what will prevent some looters or psychopaths from breaking the door down and killing us in our sleep? Or perhaps a few dozen zombies might decide to bash their way inside and turn us into their next meal? Or what if someone decides to torch these buildings with us inside? Are things starting to clear up and make sense to your satisfaction now PRIVATE JONES?"

I suddenly realized how tired I really was and how stupid I just sounded. Why hadn't I thought of that? I decided to try once again to hide my embarrassment and just shut up.

All I said was, "Yes, Ma'am."

"Very well then. Let's get some rest," Cruz said to the rest of the squad while nodding at me to start my time at the watch.

CHAPTER 11

JUNE 2043

The next several weeks were pretty much duplicates of the previous. We went from house to house, destroying any undead we happened to find. We put out fires and tore down burned structures. We scavenged food, bottled water, clothing, and weapons wherever we could. We continued to build barricades around the town, closing off more of it from the outside world. It also seemed that each day more "recruits" showed up to assist with the chores.

On the Colonel's orders, we raided and cleaned out the Meggo Mart where I formerly worked. The shopping center also had a bunch of different specialty stores as well as a nearby home center. We confiscated tons of building supplies, fencing, and tools. Even though there was no electricity at that time, we stored many power tools in preparation for the day the lights came back on. In the meantime, we used hand tools to do our building. There was also an outdoor hunting store nearby, which supplied us with plenty of guns and ammunition.

We put down a ton of zombies during this time, especially at the shopping centers. It was strange that the dead seemed to be almost drawn to those places just like when they were alive. We had to have a way to get rid of the hundreds of decomposing corpses, so we set up a burn station just outside of town at the landfill. There was a flaming pyre burning 24-7, not only for the dead but also for garbage. We learned early on that it was as essential to get rid of our refuse as it was our dead. We had to do all we could to squelch the spread of disease.

Medical supplies, like everything else, were in short supply, as we're the doctors and nurses who might use them. We did what we could with what we had, and before too long, the entire town of Franksville was secure and zombie-free. Cruz had begun to appreciate my contributions, and although she still didn't seem to like me very much, she at least started trusting me. During our final weeks in town, she permitted me to return to my apartment and spend my nights there. I could understand the army's need to keep us all together during the initial crises when zombies were everywhere. It was nice to spend some time in familiar quarters and sleep in my own bed.

However, within a week of securing the final sections of the barricade, we received orders stating most of us would be leaving to assist with the next town's barriers. Some of the older recruits would stay in town to man the guard stations and deal with any new zombies that might show up when citizens died. We understood when someone died; they came back; we just didn't know why. As such, we had to put them down within seconds of their passing.

The rest of us were going to head south toward the city of Yuengsville. It was much larger than Franksville and much more densely populated. I had a feeling we were going to have our work cut out for us down there. Unfortunately, I was all too right about that.

CHAPTER 12

Our ragtag convoy of assorted vehicles wound its way down the winding portion of Route 61, connecting the Franksville area with the small town of Saint Clara. This region was one of the areas we now referred to as the outlands. Someone somewhere up the chain of command decided that any area between the fortified safe cities should carry this designation. These areas were not under the protection of the military or police. They simply couldn't be as they were too vast. Most people formerly living in suburban and rural areas were either dead, undead, or had found their way into the fortified towns.

Then again, that wasn't entirely true. There were others such as criminals and renegades who had opted to stay in the lawless outlands living their lives as they chose to rather the risk conscription and forced to adhere to civilized law. They thought of themselves as free spirits, but in reality, they were nothing more than outlaws. People coming in from the outlands seeking refuge told stories of robbery, rape, and murder at the hands of these renegades. For these Outlanders, the Z43 virus was a blessing. It allowed them to live their lives as they always wanted to, as wild savages.

It was Tuesday evening, June something or other, and the sun was just starting to set. Our caravan consisted of three army vehicles, a variety of pickup trucks, and a few of the borough's dump trucks. We had most of the trucks packed with tools, lumber, fencing, and other items helpful in building barricades. However, some carried medical supplies and weaponry.

As we neared the bottom of the hill just before the place where the curving road finally straightened out, the lead vehicle started to slow down, forcing us to all slow as well. We were third in line, the final army vehicle, and about ten of the other civilian trucks traveled behind us.

"I wonder what the holdup is," Sergeant Cruz said from the driver's seat.

Sitting in the shotgun seat was a recruit, a new guy whose name I didn't remember. I thought it might be Chuck Walters or Walker or something like that. I was in the seat directly behind Cruz, and the tough guy Al Lawson was behind the recruit. Seated between us and not at all happy about the seating arrangements was our Amazon warrior Ace Hargrove.

I assumed she would have been a lot happier sitting next to Cruz. I don't know if she was attracted to Cruz's stern demeanor, but if so, I suspected she would be disappointed. My gaydar usually works well, and I was confident Cruz was as straight as an arrow. I was surprised to suddenly realize I was hoping she was heterosexual, not that I would ever have a chance with her. She was so far out of my league she'd need binoculars even to find my league.

Cruz picked up her walkie and said, "Able 1, this is Charlie 3. Come in Able 1." There was no reply. She repeated the call, trying to reach the lead vehicle, "Able 1, this is Charlie 3. Come in Able 1." When she didn't get a response, she tried the second vehicle, "Baker 2 this is Charlie 3. Come in, Baker 2."

Suddenly the radio seemed to explode with chatter as screaming voices reverberating throughout the cab. "Oh my God, no . . . Help! . . . There's too many of them . . . ahhhhh!"

"What the hell's going on up there?" Walters or Walker said as he rolled down the window and stuck out his head to get a better look.

"Walker, no, don't!" Cruz shouted. But her shout came too late as the young recruit's body disappeared out the window. Cruz reacted quickly and grabbed onto his ankles, trying desperately to pull him back inside. The body thrashed and twisted until finally, Cruz was able to pull him back inside. That is to say; she managed to draw what was left of him back inside. As she fell back against the driver's door, Cruz realized all she had in her grip were his legs and some of the bottom half of Walker's body.

Bloody entrails flew about the cab like snakes spewing blood, bile, and stomach contents on everyone inside. The stench was incredible! As

Cruz released her grip on the legs, several long arms began to reach inside the window, grabbing her. Soon the owner of those appendages, a giant hideous zombie, stuck his head in the window, hoping to get far enough inside to grab onto this next meal.

I pulled out the thirty-eight revolver, which Cruz had issued to me several weeks earlier, and shot the creature right between the eyes. The sound inside the truck's cab was deafening, and the bullet's impact blew the monster right out the window. Cruz pushed Walker's legs onto the floor and immediately pressed the button to close the passenger window. Luckily, it closed before any more of the creatures could find their way inside.

"Thanks, DB," Cruz said. I figured that was about the most I or anyone else would get from her in the way of a compliment, especially since she called me DB and not Jones.

"No sweat Ma'am. What the hell is going on?" I asked.

Cruz looked in the rearview mirror and said, "Good. The rest of the convoy is backing up." I suddenly realized that for a time, we were sitting ducks, trapped behind the truck in front of us and the one behind us. With them backing up, we could do so ourselves and take a few minutes to figure out what we should do next. I noticed the truck in front of us was not joining us.

As the remainder of our caravan was backing up the hill, I could see what was happening to the first two vehicles. Dozens of zombies had covered the trucks. I saw the monsters pulling passengers from the trucks among futile, ineffective gunfire. The zombies tore my comrades to pieces in a savage frenzy feast of the damned.

"I've never seen so many of those creatures together in one location before. There must be fifty or sixty of them!" Cruz exclaimed, looking through a pair of field binoculars.

Then Ace said, "Please, Sergeant Cruz, we can't just sit back and let this happen."

"Don't worry, Ace, we won't," Cruz said. Then she shouted into her walkie, "All units prepare for battle. I don't want to see even one of those maggot motels standing when we're finished." She looked in the rearview mirror at us and said, "Strap in people, this ain't gonna be pretty."

I heard the roar of a dozen truck engines revving in unison as we raced back down the road toward our destiny. Our southbound roadway was a one-way two-lane separated by thick woods. The two trucks sat where the southbound and northbound roads met, giving us four lanes to navigate, although they blocked one of the lanes. In addition, zombies were staggering all over the highway.

Cruz had the pedal pressed to the floorboards as she sped toward the crowd of zombies. Our truck slammed into the mass of undead, sending them into flying bits and pieces. Our seatbelts tugged, and the truck bounced as it ran over the creatures. As we passed the crowd, Cruz pulled the truck over and shouted, "Kill 'em all."

We threw open our doors as the other trucks in our convoy pulled over and discharged their passengers, all armed to the teeth with weapons. We were all insane with fury at what had happened to our comrades. We attacked the hoard with the savagery of madmen. Arms, legs, and heads flow in every direction as bullets riddled the walking corpses. It was as though none of us cared about taking the time for headshots; we were filling the rotting meat-sacks with lead.

When the last zombie hit the ground, the area looked like a slaughterhouse. We were fortunate that our only casualties that day were those soldiers in the first two trucks, and Walker, all of whom the creatures caught by surprise. By now, it was getting darker, almost too dark to see without a flashlight. I stood in the glow of one of the truck's headlights and noticed something strange. The radiator and windows of the first two vehicles appeared to have been shot out.

I suddenly understood that somehow, these creatures had help. Perhaps someone had even herded the zombies here for this specific purpose. I noticed something spraypainted on the side of the first truck. It was a large ruby red letter "D" inside a red circle. The paint ran down the door, looking like so much blood. I reached out to touch it and was surprised to find it was still wet. I wondered not only what the logo meant but who had left it.

"Deimos," a voice said from behind me. I turned and saw Sergeant Cruz staring angrily at the symbol.

I asked, "Did, did you say Deimos, Ma'am?"

"Yes, I did, Jones. Deimos is the leader of a band of low-down, murdering Outlanders. From what I hear, he's a ruthless psychopath who murders without remorse."

"Ma'am, I believe I met this Deimos several months ago, the day after everything went to Hell."

"You did? Then please enlighten me, Jones. How did you meet him, and how did you manage to survive? Many people don't."

I reminded her, "Do you recall when we met, and I asked if you were part of the real army or some mercenary group."

"Of course," she replied, "And do you recall how I almost shot your balls off?"

"Um, uh yes, Ma'am," I said with renewed embarrassment. "Well, Deimos was one of a group of mercenaries out to make money killing zombies. They asked me to join them, but something seemed a little off with the whole group, and that Deimos character seemed especially way off, like probably nut house wacko. He didn't seem to like me very much, and he gave me the creeps."

"Well, you made the right choice Jones. From what I heard, Deimos killed their commander with the help of a few of his cronies and then took over. Had you joined up Jones, you probably would have been among the murdered."

I suppressed a gulp, knowing she was right.

"Now, Deimos commands an army of more than 100 renegades living like savages in the outlands. As I said, that's his mark there." She pointed to the graffiti on the door. "He must have lured that bunch of deadheads out here to interfere with our mission. I surprised he didn't stay to attack us himself, the stinking coward."

At first, I didn't reply. Then I said, "Deimos or his men were here at least to start the attack, Ma'am. Look at the windshield and the radiators; someone shot both of them."

"Good catch Jones. But I'm sure the cowardly scumbag is long gone by now."

I didn't reply; there was no need.

Cruz ordered some of us to stand guard, watching the nearby woods for zombies as well as Outlanders. I was unfortunately assigned to deal with my fallen comrades in the two vehicles. It was not a pleasant task. The monsters had ripped most of them to pieces and partially devoured them as well. Then, as if to add insult to injury, several had returned from the dead as zombies. They didn't pose much of a threat as they were only minimally intact corpses, but they nonetheless had to be put down. This type of assignment was never a fun task, especially when the zombies had once been your friends.

Of course, Cruz had a slogan for that as well. She noticed our reluctance to kill our former soldiers, who were now nothing but incomplete carcasses writhing on the ground with jaws snapping or trying to drag themselves toward us with half their insides slogging next to them. She said, "Remember, people, it's no longer your bud when it rises from the mud."

Yeah, you guessed it. That became Zombie Slayer Rule #3.

Eventually, when we cleaned up the mess, what remained of our convoy made it safely to Yuengsville with no further attacks. Once there, we joined forces with those recruits who were already hard at work. We spent the next several months killing deadheads and fortifying the city perimeter.

CHAPTER 13

SEPTEMBER 2043

This fortification process in Yuengsville proved to be a significantly greater challenge than securing the borders of Franksville because of the sheer size of the city. I had no idea how many dark nooks and crevices existed from which a zombie might be able to crawl out to attack. I mean, it wasn't like they were smart enough to hide and attack with any plan or strategy. It was just that sometimes they would just stumble mindlessly into an alley or some abandoned property, and then they would essentially shut down until some noise awoke them. It might be days or weeks, or God only knew how long, but eventually, something would arouse them, and they'd be back on the hunt.

During those early days, I had plenty of opportunities to observe these undead creatures in action. Despite what people said about their insatiable hunger, I don't believe that such a state existed. I suspected these monsters were never hungry at all. Why would they be? They were dead, yes reanimated dead but dead. They did not need food or nourishment, and as I said, they couldn't have an appetite. However, they could have some sort of craving, and that was one thing they certainly did have.

You see, I think once reactivated, these zombies felt some primitive need to eat. It might be the result of some genetic memory trapped somewhere deep inside their rotting minds, some force driving them to seek out warm flesh to consume. Ok, I know what you must be thinking. Maybe I've gone beyond my limited knowledge as well as my ability to understand. So let me try to keep it simple. Let's just say from my observations, although these things are dead, and I believe they do not need food, they nonetheless need to go through the motions of eating constantly, and what they prefer to eat is us.

Another thing I noticed during this time was, I was finally starting to bulk up a bit from a muscle standpoint. This muscular increase was likely from all the physical work the Army had me doing while rebuilding the towns and fortifying their borders. I also was improving my zombie-slaying techniques. In addition to my, Army-issued armaments, I had added some other weapons to my arsenal. I still had that knife from the first night of the zombie plague. I also had two katana-style blades, which I picked up somewhere along the way, much like those I had seen used by that mercenary named Razor.

I had rigged crisscross leather sheaths of sorts on my back, which held the blades quite well and gave me quick access. Yes, I realize these weren't precisely authorized U.S. Army issue armaments, but these weren't typical times by any means. Even my style of dressing had taken on a more nonconforming appearance. I had begun wearing those snakeskin boots I mentioned earlier as well as a pair of black leather pants. These weren't the same pants I had gotten during my adventures as a wannabe rock singer. I had put on some much-needed weight, and those skinny rocker days had given way to more of a renegade biker look.

My commanding officer, Sergeant Cruz, didn't mind as long as I got my work done and kept the undead body count high. I wouldn't go so far as to say she might have had any attraction to me, physical or otherwise, but things had gotten much easier between us. She now referred to me as D.B. rather than Private Jones or just Jones. It may not sound like much, but it told me I might have gained her respect if nothing else.

I remember it was early on an early September morning after muster when Colonel Deacon arrived. I thought he might have been there to give one of his impromptu morale-building speeches. God knows he had tons of them. But I was mistaken. His purpose was much more serious and important than any of us had realized. He was there to announce some new plan the government was unveiling.

"Good morning, people," he called out from atop his flatbed, "I am here to discuss not only our current situation but plans for both the immediate future as well as even further on down the road. At the time of your conscription, several months ago, we were unable to spell out exactly how many years of service we would require of you, and although we still don't know that number, there seems to be a light at the end of the tunnel as it were."

I had been as excited as everyone else in the crowd, hoping to learn how many more months or years of our lives we would have to spend in the service of our country. Unlike most of my fellow draftees, I wasn't in a hurry to return to the private sector. I felt like I had found some direction and purpose in the army. I had been doing this job since April, and here it was, early September already. We had spent the spring, and summer building walls, transporting supplies, and slaying zombies.

I was, however, becoming very concerned about the frigid winter weather coming just around the corner. What would happen to us then with no electricity or heat other than what we might squeeze out of those few homes with fireplaces? Despite the climate changes which began in the early part of the century, Schuylkill County winters were still quite cold.

Colonel Deacon announced, "The cities and towns designated by the state government for fortification have all been secured. There are, of course, other areas of Pennsylvania and other states that could benefit from our assistance. However, because of the still-evolving conditions of both state and federal governments, it has become impossible to determine the requirements of individual states at this time. In addition, Pennsylvania is about ready to institute a new program designed to help eradicate those undead remaining in the outlands."

I suddenly became interested in what the Colonel had to say. It was starting to sound to me like my comrades, and I might have the opportunity to leave the army a bit earlier than I originally had planned. I wondered what that "plan" the Colonel was referring to might be.

The Colonel said, "The Pennsylvania government is instituting a new procedure as part of an experimental pilot program. If successful, the plan will hopefully be picked up first by adjoining states such as New Jersey, Ohio, New York, and Delaware. Then eventually, it could spread nationwide."

I thought, "Alright, already get on with it. Tell us for Pete's sake."

"This program is known as DK5479-45. The purpose of the DK5479-45 program is to provide a method for rewarding citizens who destroy any of the undead they encounter. As part of the requirements for the DK5479-45 program, every Pennsylvania resident will be required to have a personalized digital code that will identify them by what was once called a social security number, presently known as a citizen number. In the event of a confirmed kill, that person will automatically receive a $100 credit in the bank account of his choice; minus the appropriate taxes, of course."

We were all salivating at the idea of such a program. After all, the Army had been responsible for turning us into highly skilled zombie slayers. My mind immediately began calculating how many deadheads I had killed during the previous months, then multiplying the total by $100 for each kill. By my calculations under this new plan, I could have made thousands of dollars.

The Colonel continued to explain, "The way it will work is fairly simple. Each citizen wishing to participate in the bounty program will be issued several markers like this one."

He held up a long thin rod that resembled some sort of antenna. It even had a spring near its base. At the top of the rod, a flag was flying, displaying a cube-shaped code.

"This code will represent your citizen number. As you can see, the bottom end of this rod has a sharp metal point. As soon as you bring a zombie down, stick this flag into the corpse at its highest point to make it easily visible. Next, you are to take a picture of the body and the flag using your communications units and forward that picture to the appropriate authorities. Once the corpse is recovered and your identity confirmed, you will receive a $100 credit in your bank account. Any questions?"

We all looked at each other with a bit of confusion until one older soldier who I didn't know asked, "Colonel Deacon, Sir?"

"Yes, Private, what is your question?"

"Sir, it was my understanding that the Communications Unit Network was down along with the internet. If that's still the case, sir, our CUs won't work. Also, there has been little electricity available which makes charging our CUs rather difficult."

There were a series of chuckles within the crowd.

"Quite true Private, which brings me to the next several points. First, as members of the U.S. Armed Forces, killing zombies is considered part of our jobs, which means we are excluded from the benefits of the DK5479-45 program."

Now there were murmurs of discontent among the troops since everyone knew we took down more zombies than all the civilians combined. I assumed they put this regulation into place partly because of our access to weapons and ammunition as soldiers. However, they also enacted it because virtually anyone who could walk and carry a gun was now part of the military. There just weren't that many civilians left who were capable and willing to tangle with the undead, mano-a-deado.

The Colonel said, "Keep in mind, people, as soon as any of you have completed your terms of service, you will be eligible to receive the benefits of the DK5479-45 program once instituted. Any other questions?"

Now he had hit on a topic that was of great interest to me. I shouted out, "Colonel Deacon, Sir. As you know, Colonel, none of us has ever been told our actual required length of service. Is there a way for us to find that out?"

"That certainly is a good question and one worthy of an answer if I had one to give. It's a bit of a paradox you see with many varied and conflicting issues. For example, we need your services to help protect our fortified cities, and we will need your help to get the electric grids, the Communications Unit Network, and the Internet up and running. So, as you can see, we can't activate DK5479-45 until we have a stable network up and running as well as a functioning electrical grid."

Now the murmurs became even more troubled and angry sounding. The crowd began to shuffle with restlessness. I started to become afraid things were going to get out of control fast. The Colonel must have sensed this as well.

He said, "Listen up, people. I understand your concerns. But rest assured, the U.S. government has no desire to keep you conscripted for longer than is necessary. The need for your various skills is as much in demand in the civilian world as it is here."

"So, when do we get out?" An unidentified voice shouted from the crowd.

The Colonel hesitated for a moment, then said, " I can't give you a definite date at this point. However, I would not hesitate to speculate that once we have electricity, Internet, and the CU Unit Network up, and running as close to how they were before as possible, then we can start looking at releasing some of you from your duties. So now, troops, I'd suggest we do all we can to restore our various utilities and communications networks as quickly as possible."

I had no idea what we had to do to make that happen, but I suspected the colonel did. As with everything else we did since this whole zombie thing started, someone with the necessary know-how would show up soon and give us grunts our marching orders, and we, of course, would do what we were told, like the good little soldiers we were. The fact was, I didn't care. All I wanted was to get through one day safely then move on to the next, all the while further honing my zombie-slaying skills. If someday it became necessary for me to put all this army life behind me, maybe I could consider starting to collect some of that zombie-killing bounty money.

Once out of the army, I assumed I could knock down at least a grand a day without even breaking out in a sweat. Those walking maggot farms were practically tripping over each other outside our protected walls. I'd supposed I must be sure to get plenty of those antenna flag thingies because someday soon, I would be making all the money I could.

CHAPTER 14

OCTOBER 2043

By the late Fall of 2043, I had what was at least the start of a goal or a life plan for the very first time in my life. If I spent whatever time I had left in the Army building up my strength and zombie-killing skills, I might be able to make an excellent living as a zombie slayer when I got out. I decided while still active; I'd volunteer for any assignment involving hunting the undead. That way, I could keep honing my techniques.

Once out of the Army, I wouldn't have to rely on finding people to hire me as a mercenary; I could just kill creatures and collect the bounty from the government. I understood this might only prove to be a moneymaker for a few years until the zombie population went the way of the dodo, but I figured what the hell, a temporary plan was better than no plan. Then again, people die every day, which meant more zombies for me to kill, and more money to earn.

I recalled my encounter with the mercenaries and that girl from the night it all started. She had called me Death Bringer. Now, that was a cool name for a zombie killer if I ever heard one. Yeah, Death Bringer Jones, Zombie Slayer. Nice, real nice. I found myself daydreaming about someday becoming a famous sword-swinging zombie slayer known worldwide. Yeah, that would be so awesome. I'd be like a real superhero.

"Private Jones," a voice bellowed from nearby, "Are you gonna stand around with your mouth hanging open and thumb up your butt all day, or are you going to do something worthwhile for a change?" It was a voice I had grown to know as well as my own.

"Sorry, Sergeant Cruz Ma'am," I replied instinctively, "Ready to do whatever the sergeant needs, Ma'am."

The rest of our squad had assembled, and I could see Cruz was about to make an announcement. She said, "Ok, people, here's the deal. I'm looking for two volunteers to accompany a group of engineers to the local electric substation. It's located in the outlands about five miles outside of town. The assignment might take you away for as long as a week. The reason I'm asking for volunteers is that this could prove to be a dangerous assignment. We've seen firsthand what sort of challenges await in the outlands. I'm not just talking about dead heads either but living Outlanders as well, and remember people; those folks like to shoot back and do so quite freely."

"I'll go, Sergeant," I said immediately. I swear I could hear a collective sigh of relief coming from the rest of the group. They probably figured if I was dumb enough to volunteer, well, more power to me.

Cruz looked at me with surprise. It was probably the first time I had ever volunteered for anything. Then again, previously, the higher-ups just told us what we needed to do and ordered us to do it. Not wanting to be outdone by a man or perhaps just by me, and not wanting to risk the chance that I might have impressed Sergeant Cruz, our resident diesel-dyke Ace Hargrove spoke up.

"Count me in as well," she said, "I'd hate to see anything bad happen to one of my comrades. I'll be happy to look after Private Jones for you, Sergeant."

Cruz gave Hargrove a nasty look as if to suggest some unspoken chick message had passed between them. I can't say for sure, but the vibe I got was that Ace was insinuating that she suspected something sexual might be going on between Cruz and me. The sarcastic way her comment slid off her snake tongue and out the side of her mouth reeked not only of disrespect but also, dare I say, jealousy.

Look, I wouldn't have minded as much if I had been partaking in what Sergeant Cruz had to offer, but I was pretty sure her interest in me never went any further than whatever I had to provide the Army. Why Ace was acting like a spurned lover was beyond me.

Unless, nope, I'd better not to go there either. No way Cruz would have ever crossed the line and hooked up with Ace. I was sure her gate didn't swing that way. Nope, I believe all of this came from some fantasy Ace dreamed up in that twisted little brain of hers.

"I assure you, Private Hargrove, Private Jones can take care of himself quite nicely."

Great, I thought; Hargrove could take that last comment two ways. Now Hargrove would most definitely believe I have something going on with Cruz. Wonderful, just freaking wonderful.

"The both of you just make sure you take good care of the technicians we're sending with you and bring them back alive. As I said, you don't only have to worry about the dead heads but living Outlanders. Just for the record, your orders regarding renegade Outlanders are the same as the undead; kill on sight. Fire first, don't bother asking questions."

I realized I just was handed another zombie slayer rule. I couldn't remember which rule number I was up to, but I'd figure it out later when I wrote it down with the others. Now I had a mission, and if Ace Hargrove didn't try to frag me in the field, I just might come back with a few more tricks of the trade.

At first, I wasn't sure how I felt about the "shoot on sight" rule applied to living human Outlanders. Then I recalled how Deimos and his gang had been responsible for the attack on our caravan. I thought about the death of some of my friends and comrades. That made the idea much easier to accept. This indeed was war, after all. As such, anyone living or undead standing in our way had to be dealt with accordingly.

Sergeant Cruz pointed to three men in coveralls standing next to a utility truck. "Ace, D.B., this is Matt Cooper, Jon Hanson, and Kurt Dawson. They are highly skilled technicians who together represent our best chance to get electricity flowing again sometime very soon. That makes each one of them more valuable than you, I, and twenty more soldiers combined. In other words, get them where they need to go, protect them while they're working, and bring them back safely. If you fail to protect them, then I'd suggest you not bother returning yourselves. I can guarantee you wouldn't be receiving a very warm welcome. Have I made myself clear?"

"Yes, Ma'am!" We both replied simultaneously.

"Very well then, soldiers; get your gear, and be ready to deploy in ten."

We did.

CHAPTER 15

Ten minutes later, we were driving through the southern gates of Yuengsville on Route 61. Ace was in the back seat with Matt Cooper and Jon Hanson. Kurt Dawson was behind the wheel, and I was riding shotgun, literally since I was carrying a shotgun on my lap at the ready. The two technicians in the back were sitting motionless and silent while Ace watched out of the left passenger window. I could tell they weren't exactly thrilled about being in this situation.

The same was true of Kurt, our driver, who stoically stared ahead, never taking his eyes off the road. He was visibly tense and looked like he was on the verge of screaming at any moment. It was clear he hadn't been out of the safety of the city walls since all this started, although I'm sure he heard all the horrible stories of life in the outlands. He slowed down and turned left onto a secondary road.

I figured maybe I should take this opportunity to try to get the guy talking. I just thought it might ease the tension a bit. "So, your name is Kurt, is that right?"

"W . . . wa . . . what?" He stammered.

"Your name? It's Kurt, right?"

"Um, y . . . yeah, it's Kurt."

"Well, Kurt, you can call me D.B., and that's Ace in the back. I can assure you; you're in good hands. We've been dealing with these creatures since all this crap started, and we know how to handle ourselves. Isn't that right, Ace?"

A condescending voice came from the back, "I know I've got things under control. I'm not exactly sure what you've been handling. But if you've been handling yourself, I don't want to know about it."

Great I thought. Now is probably the worst time for Ace to go into angry lesbo mode, but whatever. I could see increased nervousness on Kurt's face. I tried to smooth things over.

"That Ace, she's always such a kidder. Gotta love her." I wanted to reach around and put a slug between her beady gray eyes.

Kurt said, "You said your name's D.B. What does that stand for?"

"Douche Bag," Ace mumbled from the back seat. I could hear nervous snickers from the two technicians in the back seat. Kurt remained quiet, although there was the hint of a smile on his face. What could I do? I was the one who wanted to break the tension, and if being the brunt of one of Ace's bull dyke jokes was what it took, then so be it.

"Just D B," I said, avoiding the issue.

Up ahead, something was stumbling out onto the roadway. I could see it was a dead head, an average-sized man who appeared to be about thirty years old or so. He must have died within the last few days because he didn't seem to be as rotted as some of the zombies I'd seen, but there was no doubt he was a dead one.

"Hit the gas, Kurt. Run him down," I said.

"Wa . . . what? I, I can't do that."

"Sure, you can, Kurt. What does this vehicle weigh a ton? Two tons?"

"I, I . . . d . . . don't know. Maybe two."

I told him, "Kurt, my man, what you have here is a two-ton death machine. Now step on the gas, and flatten his ass, and I mean pronto!" It hit me that I had just coined my own zombie slayer rule.

With that, I grabbed the steering wheel with my left hand and put my left foot on top of Kurt's right, pressing the pedal to the floor. The truck accelerated quickly, and in just a few seconds, we felt the bump as the truck's front slammed into the zombie sending him flying further up the road. I took my foot off the gas, and the truck continued. The creature was writhing in the road ahead trying to get up, that was until we ran over him first with the front tires, then the back.

After another twenty feet or so, Kurt stopped the truck, threw open his door, leaned over, and began to puke his guts out. I could relate to his situation, having had the same reaction so many months earlier.

"Hurl away, Kurt, my man; it all comes with the territory. Next time it'll be more manageable. Then even easier after that. Before you know it, it'll just be another day at the office. "

Kurt returned to the driver's seat, closed the door, and took a few deep breaths.

"You ok to drive?" one of the technicians said from the back seat. "If not, one of us can take over. We know the way."

"No, no, I'll be all right. I'm good."

I said, "Ok then. Let's get this thing moving."

We traveled for about another mile or so, then Kurt turned right and headed up an overgrown dirt and gravel single-lane road.

"The substation is about a half-mile up this road," he explained.

After a bit, I could see a painted cement block building with the logo painted on the side reading "Pennsylvania Electric Company." As we pulled in front of the building, we noticed the leaves on the bushes in the woods surrounding the place begin to rustle as five or more zombies stumbled out of the woods and started pounding on the truck trying to get at the food supply inside, namely us.

"Oh my God! One of the techs cried from the back. "What are we going to do?"

I looked back at Ace and said, "Time to go to work, partner."

She was already on her way out the door when she said, "Number one, we ain't partners, and number two, how's about you stop talking and start killing."

With that, Ace rounded the truck's front and shoved her knife into the first zombie's skull. The monster promptly fell to the ground. We had previously decided not to use guns unless necessary because the noise would not only attract more zombies but might alert any renegade Outlanders of our presence.

I nodded to the three technicians, who were all staring wide-eyed with shock, and said, "Sorry, fellas, can't talk now there's work to be done. Can't let the lady have all the fun."

I got out of the truck, walking straight toward two approaching deadheads while simultaneously pulling out both of my katana blades. The creature to the left was possibly a male and was way too dead. To be honest, this thing was rotten beyond my expectations. Its gray and mottled flesh hung in strips from its bones, resembling bacon cooking on a hot rock.

On the right side was a second creature. It was equally as disgusting as the first, but neither as big nor as rotting. The monster looked to be only a few days' dead. Usually, I would take out the stronger of the two under such circumstances, but I realized bacon strip boy would be such a quick kill; it would be better to put him down first, allowing me time to focus on the other one. I decided to try a new move I was developing. I swung the katana blade in my right hand, cleanly severing bacon boy's noggin.

Next, I reversed directions while simultaneously bringing up the blade in my left hand, resulting in a crisscross motion. Both of my blades struck the other creature's neck, one on each side meeting in the middle and relieving the monster of its ugly head. The body collapsed to the road where it joined his friend on a heap.

"Over here, Jones," I heard Ace shouting. I turned and saw three hungry zombies had Ace pinned near a bunch of trees. Two were females, while the third was a huge hulking male.

I ran over katana blades slicing arcs in the air. I planned to take the giant creature's head off with a similar move to what I had just done. But just as I got close, the creature lifted his arms to reach me. One of my blades took off his left arm below the elbow while the other severed his right arm at the shoulder. The creature stood staring down at the places where his arms used to be; confused, and uncertain. Before it had a chance to regroup, I brought both blades back up in a parallel motion, and the monster's head went spinning through the air.

Not wasting another second, I took off the top of the head of one of the attacking females while Ace shoved her knife up through the other thing's chin and right into its brain.

"I guess that makes us even Ace," I said, "You saved my butt once, and now I just saved yours."

"Nah, I don't think so, Jones."

Then before I realized what she was doing, Ace reached behind her and pulled out another knife, but this one made for throwing. She got ready to let the blade fly. I couldn't believe Ace was going to kill me. How did she ever hope to get away with this? I looked back towards the truck, hoping there would at least be witnesses. But none of the technicians were in sight.

"You think we're even Jones, but as big a screw up as you are, we'll never be even."

She let the blade fly. It soared past my left ear, so close that I could feel its wind as it flew by. I heard a "thwap" sound followed by the noise of something huge hitting the ground. I turned to see a huge male zombie fall to the ground with the hilt of Ace's blade protruding from its eye socket.

"Looks like you owe me again, Jones," she said with a grin. "Ace 2, Jones 1. You can start paying me back by pulling that knife out of that creature's head."

"Pull it out yourself!" I grumbled, walking back toward the truck.

As I headed back to the truck, I noticed the three technicians weren't in the truck. Oh, great, I thought, now I lost the three people I was supposed to protect. Cruz would have my nut sack sliced off and dangling from her wall before all of this was over. Then I heard a God-awful deep guttural sound, and as I rounded the back of the truck, I saw my three charges bent over, hurling whatever they might have managed to consume that day. That is, except for Kurt. My boy, Kurt, had already freed himself of the day's consumptions during his earlier barf-a-rama, and by the looks of things, all he could manage during this puke-a-thon was to yak up bile and lots of yurking sounds.

I stood patiently waiting for the three to finish their business before asking, "Are you, boys, all right. You're looking a bit worse for wear."

"We'll . . . We'll be ok in a minute," the one named Matt offered.

"Yeah. Just give me a few minutes," Jon pleaded.

"No problem, gents. Just let me know when the closing ceremonies of this year's Hurl-Olympics are over."

"Oh my God!" Kurt exclaimed, wiping his mouth on his sleeve, "I honestly don't think I've ever seen anything like what you just did out there, D.B."

"All in a day's work, Kurt. It's what I do."

"It was just . . . simply incredible the way you rained death down on them."

I suggest, "Well, to be honest, they were already dead long before we got here."

"Yeah, I know, but . . . well, that was unbelievable. Thanks again, D.B. Say, when are you going to tell me what D.B. stands for anyway?"

I leaned over and said with a conspiratorial whisper, "It stands for Death Bringer, Death Bringer Jones. But don't let that get around."

I knew full well there was no way this guy would keep this a secret. First, he'd tell the other two techs, and then they would blab to their friends and relatives. You see, I was already planting the seeds for my future job as a zombie slayer once Uncle Sam decided to cut me loose. Word of mouth might get me some gigs to fill in when I wasn't collecting bounties.

"Hey. Wait a minute. I heard that name before."

"You did?" I asked. He had caught me off guard. Was someone else running around calling himself Death Bringer Jones? If so, I had to find out, and fast.

I asked, "We've never met before today, Kurt. How could you have heard that name?"

"Well, I'm not sure. Leave me think about that. I'm sure I heard it somewhere. Yeah, yeah, now I remember. There is this kid from my hometown, Franksville. His name is Jack Elders. He's about fifteen and can draw like nobody's business. He's worked up a bunch of comics about a superhero zombie slayer with the same name as yours and has been copying them and spreading them around. That why it sounded so familiar."

"But how would he know that name? He couldn't have just made it up."

"I asked him once where he got the idea for his hero, and he said a day or so after all this started, he, his father, mother, and couple others found themselves trapped near a burning building, surrounded by zombies. He was sure they were all going to die. Then out of nowhere, some guy showed up with a baseball bat and started cracking zombie skulls like coconuts. Then, some hot girl came up the street, kissed the guy, and called him

Death Bringer Jones. He said they all shook his hand and walked away, shouting his name. After that, Jack began developing his comics. They're good. He hopes to find a real publisher someday and distribute them as graphic comic books, and eventually maybe a graphic novel."

I was dumbfounded. I had no idea how to respond to that. It was surreal hearing that day recounted to me, knowing the kid had developed a comic about me who he thought of as a hero.

Kurt said, "Come to think about it, the guy in Jack's comics looks a lot like you, maybe bigger, and with more muscles, no offense. You know how these graphic novels always have larger-than-life heroes. But I tell you, there is a resemblance. Oh well, I'd better check on Matt and Jon. We have to get up the road to the substation as soon as possible."

I didn't respond, still thinking about that kid and his drawings. I'd have to make a point of tracking him down someday when I got out of the army. I was a bit overwhelmed by the idea that I was the star in the same sort of graphic novel and comic books I had spent so much of my time reading. It was way beyond cool.

CHAPTER 16

We stayed at the substation for about three days. I have no idea what Kurt, Jon, and Matt did during that time, as Ace and I spent most of our time watching out for the undead while patrolling outside. The techies would occasionally poke their heads outside to retrieve something they needed from the truck, but for the most part, I never saw them. I had parked the vehicle close to the front door, and that's where I slept at night. Ace stayed inside the building with the technicians overnight, just one of the boys. Yeah, I know, that was low, but as you may have noticed, Ace and I weren't very tight.

She did manage to answer a few of my inquiries during those three days. Unfortunately, most of her replies were an obligatory grunt or the rare "yeah" or "nah" responses. Not a significant leap forward by any means, but I felt confident she might not try to kill me, at least not in the immediate future. That didn't stop me from locking the doors to the truck at night. Also, I did my best to sleep in an unidentifiable way from anyone looking in from the outside.

On the morning of the third day, I awoke to a muffled slapping against the left rear window of the truck. I happened to be sleeping on the back seat at the time, and the annoying sound woke me up. As was my custom, I awoke immediately with my gun at the ready. Then I recalled this was supposed to be a silent mission. I put the gun back into its holster and looked up at the window through bleary eyes, hoping fruitlessly to see Ace or one of the techs banging on the window. No such luck.

As you may have guessed, it was a dead one, or I should say a cluster of dead ones. I'm not sure where they stumbled from, but it was apparent that they wanted to partake of the dinner located in the backseat of the truck, and apparently, I put the "me" in the meal.

I looked around the car and counted six of them. One by one, they approached the truck and began banging their wretched fists against the windows. I didn't think they'd be able to break the glass and get in at me, but who knew what might happen? Maybe one of them would be holding some object that he could use to break the glass. I knew they didn't have the brains to use rocks or tools to get inside, but what if, by some freak of lousy luck, one of them was holding something they could inadvertently smash their way inside?

Regardless, the constant slapping of hands and clicking of bones where they stuck through the rotting flesh was getting on my nerves. Not to mention the disgusting look of oozing puss running down the sides of the windows. This demonstration is not the sort of thing you want to see before you've had your breakfast.

I examined the situation and decided the right front door had been receiving the least attention, so that would be the spot where I would leave the truck and do what I needed to do. Speaking of which, and please forgive my bluntness, I should point out that I had to pee badly. So, the sooner I got this over with, the better. I checked to make sure my two Katana blades and my other weapons were in place, then hopped the seat, and readied myself to open the door. I waited until just the right moment and threw the door open.

One of the creatures had been approaching the door, and when it flew open, it hit the thing square in the head, splitting open its skull and knocking it backward. I wasn't sure if the blow was enough to kill the thing, but it did do an excellent job of putting it down on the ground and at least temporarily getting it out of my way. I pulled out both blades, spun around, and began savagely slicing and dicing like a ninja with a part-time job at a sushi restaurant.

Before I realized what was happening, I had made my way to the front of the truck. I had already decapitated two of the creatures there and had hacked off limbs from another. The remaining two from the left side of the car were approaching me with their arms outstretched. I simultaneously shoved both blades into the creatures' skulls through their eye sockets and withdrew them along with bits of their rotting brains.

I thought, four for four not too shabby. Then I felt something grab onto my pant leg. It was the zombie I had hit with the door. It had crawled toward me with its jaws snapping in anticipation. Behind it, the armless wonder was lurching toward me as well. Well, alright-y then. I brought my right blade down into the crawling creature's ear, where it sliced cleanly through its brain. Then I shoved the left Katana forward and into the mouth of the monster with no arms. I thought it would have been a clean kill, but I was wrong.

My aim had been a bit off, and the blade failed to sever the spinal cord. I left my other sword in the skull of the now-dead crawling creature and put both hands on the handle of the blade jutting out of the armless zombie's mouth. I twisted the knife left, and right watching its razor-sharp edge turn the creature's mouth into some obscene oversized clown mouth. I felt and heard a cracking sound as the spine finally broke while I twisted the blade. The monster dropped to the ground as my blade slid cleanly out of its face.

I turned, and pulled my other blade from the ear of the other zombie, and thought, "Six for six. Much better."

That was when I heard a gasp and someone shouting, "Holy crap. I swear to God I've never seen anything like that in my life."

It was the three technicians standing just outside the entrance to the substation. They were all staring at me with their mouths hanging open in apparent disbelief. Behind them, Ace stood watching with an expression I couldn't exactly read. At first, I thought it might be admiration for what I had just done, and then I wasn't so sure. It looked like she might be a bit disappointed. About what, I wasn't sure. Since I didn't know how long they were standing back there, I had no idea if she had been waiting to see if the zombies would kill me or if she had just arrived and missed most of the show.

She must have read the confused look on my face because she said, "Nice work Jones, sorry I missed the fun."

However, the technician, Kurt, gave her a strange look. It made me realize they had all been there in plenty of time to act, but she had just chosen not to. Well, I suppose that answered that question. What better way to kill me off than to stand by and do nothing while a bunch of maggoty munchers chomped me to bits? I only hoped that was the last I would have to deal with Ace Hargrove. I had plans to say something to Cruz when we back and tell her I was through partnering with Ace. If she pushed the point, I'd express my suspicions, and I was pretty sure she'd agree with me, especially since Ace had made it obvious how she had felt about me before this assignment through her relentless, sarcastic comments.

"Well then, who's up for breakfast?" I said with enthusiasm.

That was when Jon passed out, and Matt fell to the ground, barfing his guts out. Kurt just stood looking at me with an expression of unconcealed awe.

Ace said, "Kurt. Look after Jon, and as soon as Matt finishes hurling, perhaps we can be on our way. You guys are all done in there, right?"

"Y . . . yeah," he stammered, "We just need to pack up our gear, and we can head back. The south side of Yuengsville should have full-electric power now."

"Southside? Not the whole city?" I asked.

He said, "No. Unfortunately, several other substations provide power to the city, and we'll have to get them up and running as well. There's another team of techs out there doing what we just did, and depending upon their level of success, we still may have a lot more work to do."

Ace mumbled, "Freakin' wonderful."

I said, "No problem Kurt. Whatever it takes to get the city back up and running, your US army will be there to do the job."

Kurt said, "I'm glad you feel that way, Dea . . . I mean D.B."

I glanced at Ace, seeing if she noticed Kurt's almost slip up, but she hadn't. I don't know why I cared whether she knew about the whole Death Bringer thing; it's just that I felt the need to have her know as little about me as possible. Bottom line, I never trusted her very much before, and now I didn't trust her at all.

"Good to hear," I said, "Now, let's get everything packed up and get ready to move. There might be more of these scumbags roaming about these woods."

CHAPTER 17

We began our trek back to the city after a hearty breakfast. To my surprise and the gratitude of our three technicians' full stomachs, we didn't run into any zombies to slay during the drive out to Route 61. However, about two miles from the southern gate of Yuengsville, we did encounter a problem of another kind.

Kurt was behind the wheel, and I was back at my post on shotgun.

"What the?" Kurt mumbled as he began to slow the truck.

I said, "What is it, Kurt, my man? You gotta know it's not safe to stop out here. Our goal should be to keep moving."

He sat staring, mouth agape, "Look up there. Ahead. What the hell is going on?"

I looked out the windshield and saw plumes of smoke billowing up from the road ahead. As I traced the smoke down to its point of origin, I could several vehicles ablaze, completely blocking the highway.

"Woah, that can't be good," Jon said from the back seat. I thought, talk about Mr. Obvious!

"You figure that out all by yourself?" Ace said smugly, "I guess that's why you're the highly skilled technician, and we are just two lowly grunts."

"So, what is it?" Matt asked.

I said, "Bad guys, criminals, Outlanders, and by the looks of that flaming roadblock, they've been expecting us."

"Why us?" Kurt asked. We have nothing they might want, do we?"

"I beg to differ," I suggested. "We have three techs capable of figuring out how to make electricity available in the outlands. That makes you three precious commodities."

"What about you and Ace?"

"Well . . . let's just say since we're the only thing standing between them and you, we're not on the top of their Christmas list."

"We're expendable," Ace said matter-of-factly. "They'll do their best to kill us to get to you three."

I said, "That's if we're lucky. If not, those maniacs will likely capture us then torture us for several days before eventually beheading us or subjecting us to some other twisted death ritual. And they'll probably rape Ace many times over before they're through."

"Um . . . what makes you think your skinny backside is going to skip violation?" She asked.

"Point taken," I said, recalling that first night of the zombie outbreak and that psycho who almost turned me into his love pin cushion.

"So, what are we gonna do?" Jon asked from the back seat.

I said, "We're going to do the only thing we can do. We're going straight through that flaming barricade."

"We are?" Kurt asked, staring out through the windshield with a look of complete disbelief on his face. "B . . . but I, I . . . c . . . c . . . can't get through that."

"Not a problem, amigo. You won't have to. I'll be driving," I announced, "Now, let's switch places."

Kurt didn't waste a second hesitating. He threw open his door and was around to my side before I even got out. I walked around and took my place behind the wheel. As I fastened my seat belt, I reminded my passengers to buckle up. Ace reached into her travel bag and pulled out two 9 mm handguns. She gave one to Jon at the rear left window and handed another to Kurt in the front passenger seat. I already had my gun in my hands.

Matt asked, "What about me? Don't I get a gun?"

"No, you don't," Ace said, "You're in the middle between us two, and I don't want you accidentally blowing our heads off."

"But what if either of you get killed?"

Ace said, "If that happens, you're more than welcome to take my gun. If I don't get shot in the head, you'll probably want to put a round in my ear, so I don't come back, and try, and chomp on you."

I heard nervous chuckling from the three technicians and decided I had better get things rolling before the Outlanders attacked us. I assumed some of them were already flanking us in the nearby woods in case we tried to turn around and make a break for it.

I was hoping to gain the element of surprise by doing something they never expected. I was sure the Outlanders wouldn't anticipate me making a head-on frontal attack. Besides being an insane idea bordering on suicidal, I also knew that it might just be crazy enough to work. Besides, if we were going to die, we might as well go out fighting. Die with our boots on, as the old 20th-century cowboy movies used to say.

Pressing my pedal to the floor, I shouted over the roaring engine, "Shoot at anything moving. Don't take a second to think; just shoot everything. We just might make it through this yet."

I shouted a war-whoop, and as the car sped toward the blazing roadblock, I noticed a tiny space of about four feet between two of the burning vehicles off toward the right side of the highway. If I could position the truck just right, I might be able to ram my way through the flaming metal hulks. I shouted, "Prepare to crash, people, we're going in!"

There were simultaneous shouts of, "Hell yeah!" accompanied by hoots and what I swear were growls. Whatever the case, I felt much more confident knowing these folks were behind in my decision. Even Ace seemed to agree, although it was hard to tell as she exuded pure bloodlust at the thought of battle.

We hit the opening with our truck focused mainly on the smaller vehicle to the left of the entrance. The impact was so great; I felt like my teeth were going to vibrate out of my mouth. Grunts and groans poured from my passengers, but we had done it; our truck was through the barrier. A shower of flaming debris fell upon our truck as we sped on. Then the bullets came.

"Return fire!" I screamed as loudly as possible. From all around me, I heard the ear-piercing reports of gunfire as my passengers returned gunfire at a rate the Outlanders had never expected. Although I tried to stay focused on getting us out of there as quickly as possible, I saw dozens of outlaws mowed down by our gunfire.

The left-side rear bumper became entangled with something on the car we had bashed. We were still moving forward but at a much slower pace since we had spun the car around and dragged it behind us.

I shouted, "Hang on!" I slammed on the breaks, allowing the car to slide toward us. Then I twisted the steering wheel to the right and floored it. As I had hoped, when I slammed on the breaks, the car slid upward off our bumper. Changing directions at a rapid speed allowed me to break free. It also had another positive although gruesome outcome. Swerving to the right and trying desperately to regain control of the truck, I didn't see a cluster of Outlanders who had just positioned themselves to fire on us. The truck not only slammed into all of them but traveled over the top of most of them.

"Oh, that's not gonna be pretty," Ace said.

Not having time to worry about such things, I once again pressed the gas pedal to the floor, and as my companions launched another barrage of bullets behind us. To this day, I have no idea if they hit anything else as we sped away or even if any Outlanders remained to fire at us. The important thing we were heading up Route 61 and were unstoppable.

Five minutes later, we were entering the southern gate of what had once been Yuengsville. However, it now bore a sign that read, "Welcome. You are entering the Yuengsville Free Zone.", and what was even more pleasing to see were lights; not candles or torches but actual electric lights.

"I turned to Kurt and said, "Kurt, Jon, Matt. You boys did good."

"So did you, Death Bringer Jones, so did you," Matt replied.

I didn't bother looking back to see if Ace had heard what he said. As far as I was concerned, she and I would not be doing any more team exercises any time soon so she could think whatever she wanted.

CHAPTER 18

As we drove through the southern gateway, I heard a series of congratulatory whoops, and cheers from the guards manning the walls. At first, I wondered why they were cheering. I had forgotten about the restored electricity. After so many months in the dark, they had reason to celebrate. We drove straight to the southern army post, and as we got closer, I saw both Sergeant Cruz and Colonel Deacon waiting for us flashing million-dollar smiles.

I got out of the truck and walked purposefully over to the pair, with Ace following a few steps behind me, trying her best to catch up. I gave a crisp salute and said, "Privates Jones, and Hargrove reporting Sirs. I am happy to report mission accomplished with no personnel casualties Sirs."

Hargrove issued a feeble sounding, "Mission accomplished, Sirs."

I thought, "If you ain't the lead dog, the scenery never changes." I suppressed a smile, but not before Cruz saw it and gave me a stern don't-you-screw-this-up look.

Colonel Deacon said, "Excellent indeed, Privates. As you can see, we now have electricity restored in this portion of the city with other sections likewise to follow soon. Again, excellent job. I suppose I should ask if you had run into any problems out there while protecting our technicians?"

"We did encounter small clusters of undead on several different occasions, but we were able to dispatch them without incident, Sir."

"And Outlanders? Did you have any problems with them? We noticed smoke rising over the mountains south of here. We were concerned it might be those savages. I was considering sending out troops right before we heard you were coming through the southern gates."

"We did have some issues, Sir. Outlanders temporarily impeded our progress by erecting a barricade of flaming on our return trip. It was obvious they were bent on kidnapping our technicians and likely killing us. I don't believe they anticipated the ferocity of our response to their attack, Sir. I drove the truck through a small opening in the barricade, while Private Hargrove and our three technician friends returned fire, killing most of the renegades."

The Colonel looked back at the three technicians standing several feet behind us. They stood looking around uncomfortably, unsure of what they should do. I knew they, too, were conscripted into the army, but it was apparent they had never actually been made to behave like soldiers, nor had they ever had to go into battle before that morning.

"Good job, gentlemen. Not only did you manage to get us electricity, but you rose to the task of defending our way of life as well."

I explained, "Unfortunately, due to the circumstances, Sir, I regret to report we were unable to take steps to assure the dead would not return."

"Not a problem Private Jones. Those dead are outside our walls, and to be honest, it gives me a good feeling knowing those living Outlanders will at least have to deal with their people returning as deadheads."

I thought of a potential problem I hoped the government had considered. I asked, "I was wondering, Sir, won't the Outlanders attempt to damage or sabotage the flow of electricity?

He replied, "Good question, Private Jones. I asked that same question. The government believes we are in no danger of that happening. For the immediate future, we will be sending out patrols to walk along the power line trail making sure no one screws with our power supply. Very soon, we'll be instituting something we call The Systematic Expansion Program, starting with the zones where our powerlines run.

"Systematic Expansion? May I ask what that is, Sir?" I inquired.

He said, "Absolutely Private Jones. Now that we have fortified this city to protect it from invaders, we need to begin expanding the perimeter of our living space. We'll put together teams of workers; some will be responsible for clearing land and installing fencing while others will be on hand to destroy zombies and kill any savages that are stupid enough to get in our way. Once the area is secure and clear, it will become part of the city. We'll expand out to the power stations like the one you just visited. When they are all cleared, we'll begin expanding the city in every direction, creating an even larger safe zone for survivors."

"But won't the Outlanders fight back like they tried to do today?"

He smiled slyly and said, "We certainly hope so, Private Jones. We certainly hope so."

The Colonel nodded to Cruz, who said, "I'd like to offer my thanks for a job well done. Now feel free to go clean up, and get some well-deserved rest."

I said, "Thank you, Ma'am," and hesitated for a moment before turning to leave. I made eye contact with Cruz and sensed she knew I had more to tell her.

She called, "Private Jones?"

"Yes, Ma'am?"

"After you've had a chance to rest up, please stop by my office," she said.

My mental message must have hit a bullseye. I wanted to meet with Cruze immediately. However, I was beyond exhausted from our encounter, and I could tell Cruz wished to speak to me alone. Any conversation I was to have with her would have to wait until after I was well-rested, and both Ace Hargrove and Colonel Deacon were well out of earshot. I noticed Ace looking over at Cruz and me. At the time, I hadn't known she had overheard our conversation. I should've realized right then she had something up her sleeve, but I was exhausted and couldn't wait to get as far away from that woman as possible.

CHAPTER 19

Several hours later, I awoke after my well-deserved nap. I had been dreaming about my parents, and not for the first time since all this zombie crap started. They had died together in a car accident two years earlier. At the time, I, of course, had been devastated. But looking at how the world turned out, it was probably for the best.

In my dream, my dad and I were sitting in their living room talking about something that I couldn't recall. Mom walked in with a plate of her amazing chocolate chip cookies and a glass of milk. I remembered asking them, "Why aren't you guys dead anymore?"

Mom replied, "We got bored with it and decided to come back for a while."

Yeah, I realize how stupid that sounds, but in dreams, all sorts of ridiculous things seem to make sense. This scenario is one I experienced often. In the light of day, I chalked it up to my subconscious using my dreams to tell me something my conscious mind was missing. Anyway, when my folks came to visit me in my sleep, it all seemed perfectly normal to me.

Dad said, "I wanted to let you know change is coming, but that doesn't mean it's a bad thing. It just means you might have to point yourself in another direction, the road you're supposed to follow."

I didn't understand what he meant. People always seem to speak in riddles in my dreams as well. Because I always wanted my parents to be proud of me, I told him that he and Mom had nothing to worry about. I explained how I was becoming a big success with the army. But before I had the chance to see their reaction, they were both gone, and I was awake. As was typical, I had forgotten about the dream. I assumed it would likely come back to me later. They often did.

I showered, got dressed, and walked over to Sergeant Cruz's office feeling more than a little overconfident. I mean, seriously, this last assignment was a home run, a slam dunk, or any other sports analogy you might want to consider. I had every right to be positive, maybe even a bit arrogant. I was the shining star, a force to be reckoned with. As I knocked on her door, I heard a little voice in the back of my mind. It was my mom repeating one of her favorite expressions.

"Delbert, overconfidence is the feeling you have right before you make the worst mistake of your life." To this day, I wonder how my life might have turned out differently if I'd heeded that warning, which of course, me being me, I didn't.

"Come in. It's open," Cruz responded. At the time, I didn't notice the touch of coldness lying just below the surface in Cruz's voice.

I entered, snapped a salute, and said, "Private Jones reporting as requested, Ma'am."

"At ease Private Jones. Have a seat," she said, nodding toward a nearby chair.

Cruz was sitting behind a makeshift desk consisting of two well-worn short file cabinets with a flat door lying across them. Stacks of paperwork covered the top of the desk. The office itself was not very spacious. I assumed correctly that Colonel Deacon had taken the more prominent space for himself and left this room for Cruz. Rank does have its privileges. When I looked back, Cruz was silently staring at me as if waiting for me to say something.

After a bit, she said, "What is it, Jones? What was it you wanted to tell me that you felt you couldn't say in front of Colonel Deacon?"

I explained, "Ah, so you did notice. Well, to be honest, it wasn't Colonel Deacon I was concerned about."

"It was Ace, wasn't it?"

"Yes, Ma'am. It was Ace."

"Look, D.B. I know you and Ace don't see eye-to-eye on a lot of things, but you have to admit, you made a good team and completed your last mission successfully."

"Well, Ma'am. It's not so much that we succeeded because of each other but despite each other. The truth is the success of this mission was because of me. Ace was more of a hindrance than a help. I felt like I had to watch my back constantly. She hates my guts, and I don't feel like I can trust her. You know the first-hand, Ma'am; trust is critical for us to do what we need to do."

She hesitated for a moment then asked, "Did Ace have an occasion to save your life out there?"

This statement made me sense something about this discussion was starting to go very wrong. The conversation had taken a turn in a direction I hadn't expected. Somehow Ace had beaten me to the punch. She must have gotten there before me and told Cruz how she had pulled my bacon out of the fire. She was no doubt trying to make herself look good in Cruz's eyes and maybe make me look bad at the same time. I decided honesty was the best policy, especially when someone asks a question and already knows the answer.

"Ma'am. We both saved each other out there. It was what was required to get the job done," I said.

Cruz looked carefully at me and suggested, "So despite the animosity, you two seem to express for each other, out in the field, where it matters, you had each other's backs. Is that not, correct?"

"Um. Yes, Ma'am, I suppose that was correct, at least this time."

"What does that mean, Private Jones, this time?"

By the tone of her voice and the fact that she had gone back to calling me Private Jones, I could tell that she was not happy with me or that response.

"Well, Ma'am," I said, "This time, it was just Ace and me in a dangerous situation. To succeed and get back alive, we had to work together as a team. She couldn't afford to let me get killed or risk fragging me without endangering herself."

"Do you honestly think so little of Private Hargrove, Jones? Do you believe she would try to kill you?"

I said with confidence, "Yes, Ma'am, I most certainly do believe she would. If we were out there with several troops in a skirmish with undead or Outlanders, I believe she would wait for the right opportunity to either let me get killed or do it herself."

"I'm shocked to hear you say that Private Jones, especially after Ace had taken it upon herself to stop by earlier and compliment your exemplary performance during the assignment."

I was blown away by this revelation, "W . . . w . . . What? I can't believe that!"

"Are you calling me a liar Jones?"

I was stepping into it now. I had no idea what Ace was up to, but she had ulterior motives if she came in here singing my praises.

I said, "No, Ma'am. Not. I'm just confused by Ace's actions. It's clear she hates me, and I wouldn't trust her as far as I could throw her. I came here to request that I not be teamed up with Ace anymore. She wants me dead; I'm certain. I have no idea why she would pretend otherwise. That is, of course, unless she's lying to get in your good graces."

"And why would she want to do such a thing?"

Without taking time to think, I blurted out, "Because she's hot for you! You've got to know she's a bull dyke, and she looks at you like you're a well-seasoned pork chop!"

Sergeant Cruz's face began to redden, and her eyes blazed with an anger I hadn't seen in a long time. She shouted, "Private Jones! You seem to have forgotten you are addressing your superior officer! I have a good mind to bring you up on charges of insubordination! What have you got to say about that?"

I hung my head down, avoiding those angry eyes, and said, "Begging the Sergeant's pardon, I meant no disrespect. I misspoke out of my anger with Private Hargrove, Ma'am. I'm most grievously sorry and hope the Sergeant will accept my apology."

"You know what, Jones? I've about had it with you. Every time I start to think you might have a place in this army, you go off and do or say something to show me just how wrong I can be. I don't believe you'll ever fit in, Jones. You're too much of a lone wolf, a renegade. You just don't know how to conform to any organized environment. I suspect that was the reason the old army rejected you before all this zombie stuff started happening. You're a misfit, a reject."

I figured I had better find a way to calm her down. I said, "You're correct, Ma'am. I've had trouble adjusting to the army way since day one. But begging the Sergeant's pardon, I've been doing my best to fit in and to get along, even with Ace. But I must admit, it's been a challenge, Ma'am."

"Well then, Private Jones, I suppose I have some good news for you."

"Ma'am? I don't understand. Good news? What good news?"

"Colonel Deacon told me today to look at my people and come up with one or two who don't quite fit well with what we're trying to accomplish here. He told me to discharge them back into civilian society. You, Private Jones, are my choice."

"Me? I, I don't understand. You mean I'm going to be discharged?"

Suddenly I was simultaneously flooded with a variety of emotions. On the one hand, I was happy to be going back to my non-military life, but on the other hand, I realized I no longer had a job or any idea how to feed myself. For the past months, Uncle Sam had provided me with everything I needed to survive. Not only did the army provide food, shelter, and medical services, but it also gave my life direction for the very first time.

If I left the army, I would be free to pursue my dream of being a famous zombie slayer, but wasn't that all just another one of my many fantasies? Even in a world as bizarre as this one had become, the idea of my becoming some sort of comic book superhero was ridiculous. I was no one special. Without the army, I'd just be an unemployed customer service representative for a store that was as dead as most of the human population.

Where would I live, back at my old apartment in Franksville? Maybe I could unless, of course, someone else was living there. A lot had likely changed since I left there to come to Yuengsville, and how would I get back? I had no transportation, and Franksville was several miles north through the wild outlands. Travel was dangerous enough in military vehicles. How could I hope to survive on foot?

"I can see you're thinking about what it's going to be like in this brave new world without the resources of Uncle Sam behind you. Well, very soon, you're going to find out first-hand what it's like to be a lone wolf.

But then again, that shouldn't be a problem for a master zombie slayer like Death Bringer Jones, should it?"

Suddenly, everything was starting to make sense. I now knew for sure why Ace had raced to see Cruz before me. She had overheard Matt, the technician, call me Death Bringer. She probably realized that although Cruz was starting to trust me more each day, it would only take someone casting enough of a shadow of doubt for her to change her mind about me. No doubt, Ace had done everything in her power to make me appear like some arrogant, egomaniacal superhero wannabe. Tossing out the name Death Bringer no doubt tipped the scales of Cruz's opinion against me.

The worst part was since I had no idea Ace had made the play she did, she put me in an impossible spot. Anything I said now against Ace would just make me look worse. I'd be coming across like some know-it-all who had the arrogance to tell his superior officer how to run her squad. No matter what I said, I'd sound like a jerk. Ace set the trap, and I fell into it face-first.

"Please, Ma'am, Sergeant Cruz. Just give me another chance. I'm sure I can change for the better. You know how much I wanted to be part of this. Let me try again to make it work," I pleaded.

"Sorry private citizen Jones, that ship has sailed. As of this moment, you are on your own. I will allow you one thing. There's a supply truck heading to Franksville in one hour. It leaves from the northern gate. I suggest you be on it."

"But . . . but can't I stay here in Yuengsville? I mean, civilians are living here now?" I asked.

She looked at me with disappointment and said, "Not gonna happen, Jones. You need to get back to your hometown. There's no place for you here anymore."

I lost my temper and growled, "You mean no place where you can see me, don't you, Samantha? Hey, if I'm out of the army, I don't have to call you Ma'am or Sergeant Cruz anymore. Yeah, maybe this won't be so bad after all. What do you think, Sammy?"

"Easy Delbert," Cruz demanded with blazing red-rimmed eyes. "One more comment like that, and your free ride up the mountain is off the table. I won't hesitate to have my soldiers toss you right out the gate into the wilderness immediately. Then you can see just how special your Death Bringer persona is. My men are going through your bunk and relieving you of all your weapons as we speak. Any guns you had were and are the property of the U.S. Army. I planned on letting you keep your Katana blades, but if you continue to piss me off, you'll be walking through the outlands, up the mountain in your underwear with not even a pen knife to protect you. Do I make myself clear?"

She most certainly had. So, my last act as a former soldier was to shut my mouth, gather my meager belongings, head to the north gate, and catch a supply truck to Franksville. I thought maybe Ace Hargrove might be waiting there to gawk as I left, but she wasn't. No one was there except the truck driver, and as far as he knew, I was just another civilian catching a ride.

"Are you Delbert Jones?" He had asked as I approached. He had a clipboard in his hands and was waiting to check my name off whatever list he had.

I thought for a moment, then replied, "Yes, that right. I'm just plain old ordinary Delbert Jones." I road the rest of the way in silence, not knowing what the next day would bring.

CHAPTER 20

As luck would have it, I found it pretty much the way I had left it when I got to my apartment. No one was currently living there, although I could tell various people might have crashed there for a night or so during the past seven months. Most of the food in my cabinets was gone, along with some of my clothing. All things considered, after some minor repairs, the place would be ready for me to move back in.

Old Mrs. Willingham's place was in ruins, completely gutted by fire, but since it was a solid brick building, I figured at some point, somebody might be able to rebuild the inside. I considered since I had nothing but spare time now, maybe I'd take on the job myself. If I could scrounge up the lumber and other supplies, I could try to figure out how to bring that old wreck back from the dead.

Before getting drafted, I didn't know much about carpentry, plumbing, electricity, or construction, but I had become reasonably proficient at the building trade, thanks to Uncle Sam. I would have to learn the plumbing and electricity as I went along, but Franksville still lacked power or running water, so I had plenty of time to learn. Maybe I could hook up with someone who could teach me what I needed to know. Regardless, I still had my apartment, which would serve me just fine as long as I needed it.

I investigated the living room, recalling that first night of the zombie apocalypse, and noticed something I'd missed when I first came in. My TV was gone. Somebody had stolen my nonfunctional TV, leaving the digital signal wires lying on the TV stand. Seriously? Why in the world would anyone bother stealing a TV in a world with no television service?

Sure, someday, service would be back, but that would likely be a long time in the future. Besides, that TV was a piece of crap anyway. I bought it used from like the third owner. I was beyond stunned. It just goes to show you how little I understood my fellow man back in those days. Not to suggest I'm a much better judge of character these days either.

I spent the remainder of the day and the next two days getting my apartment cleaned, organized, and secured. Luckily, I brought some food and water back from Yuengsville with me and figured I'd be ok for a week. Regardless, I knew I had to find myself some job in the next few days. Too bad the government wasn't ready yet to start up that bounty program. It would be awesome to collect money for doing what I loved to do and was pretty good at doing. This realization made me understand that I would have to find a way to keep up my zombie-slaying skills as well.

I decided it was time for me to venture out into the town and see what sort of job I might be able to find. As I walked around, I saw many help-wanted signs for store clerks, laborers, handymen, and dozens of other jobs I knew I could do, but none I wanted to do. It had only been a half year or so earlier; I was bored stiff working at my customer service job. Since the apocalypse started, I was right in the thick of action practically daily. I was in no hurry to give that up. I'll admit the adrenaline rush was as addicting as almost any drug, except for maybe Braino. That crap was supposed to be nasty stuff.

Going back to some tedious, mundane job might be a fate worse than death or even undeath. I thought of Sergeant Cruz, and understood she must have figured that out about me as well, which was why ending my army career was such a devastating punishment. I supposed if I had no choice, I could take on one of these regular jobs for a while, but I would most definitely only do so after all other avenues were no longer available to me.

That was when I saw the sign hanging on the outside of the door to the town hall. It read, "Security help wanted for Potential Systematic Expansion Program. Apply inside the town hall office."

"Systematic Expansion," I said to myself, recognizing the name. That was that program Colonel Deacon had been talking about the other day.

That was the system they developed to expand the size of cities by taking back sections of the outlands and clearing those areas of Zombies and Outlanders. I wondered what sort of security help they might need, even though I was sure I already knew. I found my way to the town hall and walked in to find out where I could apply.

CHAPTER 21

"May I help you?" An elderly woman said in a gravelly voice from behind a glass partition as she slid a panel sideways. A nameplate read "Edna Mortimer, Receptionist." In her late seventies, she appeared to be rail-thin with wispy white hair teased in a feeble attempt to cover her bald spot. She had a lit cigarette dangling from the right side of her mouth, forcing her to speak out of the left side. Smoke rose and caused her right eye to close slightly. If she were a man wearing a sailor cap, I would have said she looked like that cartoon character I had once seen in a museum from back in the early-20th century. I believe the character's name was Poppie or Pappy or something like that. No, it was Popeye, Popeye, the sailor. Yeah, that was it.

Holding back my laughter, I said, "Um . . . ah . . . yes, Ma'am. I'm interested in applying for the security position for the Systematic Expansion Unit."

"Oh, ya are, are ya?" She looked at me suspiciously with that Popeye face, and to be honest, with that raspy smoker's voice, she sounded like him too.

"Um . . . yes, yes, Ma'am," I replied, trying desperately not to start laughing.

"Well, what sort of experience do you have, Sonny? You ever kill any of those walking meat-sacks?"

I was surprised by her direct demeanor, but I supposed there was little time to worry about politeness in this brave new world. This woman was all business.

I said, "Yes, Ma'am. I was just honorably discharged from the U.S. Army last week, and I have personally put down hundreds of the undead, myself."

"Oh, ya have, have ya?" She inquired, "So what are you saying? Are you trying to tell me you're like some sort of big-time zombie slayer or something? What, you think you're a zombie hunting superhero like that Death Bringer Jones character?"

"Did you just say Death Bringer Jones?"

"Yeah. Of course, I did. Don't ya have any culture?" She reached under the counter and brought up a home-grown version of a comic book. It looked like someone might have taken an original version and photocopied it. But I knew that wasn't likely since there was no electricity.

"Where did you get that?" I asked curiously.

"There's a bunch of these, all around town. A local boy drew them and found someone to make him copies. Not sure how all that works, but there is a print shop in town, so they must have some way of doing it. Anyways, everybody in town loves these comics, and from what I heard, they're even finding their way to other towns."

"Mind if I take a look?"

"Suit yourself."

I picked up the comic and was amazed at the quality of the artwork. That kid could draw. This comic must have been the first episode because it recounted where I encountered the people trapped near the burning building. The artist took quite a lot of liberty in his portrayal of me, as the comic Death Bringer was quite a bit larger than I was and a hell of a lot more muscular.

The comic was quite gory and graphic, with Death Bringer Jones wielding a baseball bat and cracking open one zombie skull after another. The pages dripped with black and white images of blood splatter. At the end of the battle, a beautiful woman approached and kissed Death Bringer on the lips. I assumed that was supposed to be the grateful woman I had saved from the rapist, but she was barely dressed in the comic, and massive breasts spilled from her scant clothing. Pen and ink can be a dangerous tool in the hand of a hormonal teenager. No wonder this was such a popular comic book.

A gruff voice said, "So are ya gonna stand there gawking at the comic book all day, or do ya want to apply for the job?"

I was startled back to reality, "Um, yes, I'd like to apply."

"Well, then take this here form, sit down over there, and fill it out." She handed me a clipboard with a document attached and a pen on the end of a long string.

"Lose a lot of pens, do you?" I asked with a sarcastic smile.

"Not since I tied them to a string," she replied smugly, "Now either fill out the form or leave. Either way is fine with me."

As I studied the form, I saw the first line asking for the applicant's last, first, then middle names. I considered writing Jones, Death, Bringer in the spaces provided, but I didn't think I wanted to get into all that with this female Popeye, not if I wanted to land the job. So, I put Jones, Delbert, Bertram and continued to fill out the rest of the form. When I finished, I handed it to the not-so-pleasant woman. She read the first line and looked at me scornfully.

"Jones, is it? Sounds like a fake name to me, and Delbert Bertram? Seriously? Couldn't your parents do better than that?"

I had about enough of this woman by this point and said, "Look, lady, and I use that term loosely; my name is Delbert Bertram Jones. It's the name my parents gave me, and as such, I'm stuck with it. My friends call me DB, but you can call me Mr. Jones since you don't qualify. Now, who do I talk to about the job, preferably somebody other than you."

She looked at me for a moment without speaking and then said, "Well ya don't have to get your panties in a bunch over this, Mr. Jones. I'm just doing my job. Now, if you'll be kind enough to go over there and sit for a minute, I'll have my supervisor, Mr. Elders, speak to you shortly."

I walked over, and plopped down into one of the molded plastic chairs, and stewed for a while, waiting for the boss to arrive. I usually didn't lose my temper so quickly. Still, I was just frustrated with this woman's attitude, especially considering she had no idea the person she was giving crap was her favorite comic book hero. The entire situation was just too weird for me to comprehend, and where had I heard that name Elders before?

A few minutes later, the receptionist returned to her desk and called over to me, "Mr. Jones. Mr. Elders would like to see you in his office now."

I got up and crossed over to a hallway next to the reception desk.

"It's the second door on your right," the receptionist said coldly.

The hall was dark, and I could see the light coming from an open doorway, the second on my right. I assumed it must have many windows since any area without windows like the hall was completely dark. As I turned to the right and entered the room, natural daylight coming in through a wall behind the desk temporarily blinded me. As my eyes adjusted, I saw a man sitting behind the desk, his backlit face unrecognizable in shadows. I carefully stepped forward, walking into the room, displaying more confidence than I felt.

"Death Bringer Jones. Is it really you?" The man's voice said.

CHAPTER 22

I was more than a little confused over his greeting. Who was this Elders guy anyway, and how did he know me? Not to mention, how did he know me as Death Bringer?

"Excuse me?" I said in honest-to-goodness confusion. "What did you just call me?"

"Death Bringer Jones," he replied, "Master zombie slayer, fearless hero, and star of my son Jack's graphic comics."

"Son Jack?" I thought. Then I remembered where I had heard the name before. Matt, the electrical technician, mentioned Jack Elders as the kid drawing the Death Bringer comics.

"But what makes you think that's me," I asked, not sure why I did other than to buy myself some time to figure out where all this was going.

The man leaned forward into the light, and his face became both visible and somewhat recognizable. It took me a few seconds to recall where I had seen him before. He had been the older gentleman who was among the crowd of people I helped save that morning shortly after the apocalypse had begun. Suddenly it was all starting to make sense to me. The boy I saved had created the superhero comic version of me, and this man was his father.

"You," that was all I managed to say.

"Yep, me," he replied, "It's been a while since that day you saved our lives."

"Well, to be honest," I said, not trying to sound humble but just stating the truth, "I may have gotten the party started, but you folks all chipped in and did your part as well."

"Maybe so, but had you not intervened and inspired us to fight back, we would have died for sure, and for that, I'm eternally grateful. You not only showed initiative but natural leadership ability. So, it seems apparent today is your lucky day, Death Bringer. I need men like you on my Systematic Expansion team, and I always repay my debts. As far as I'm concerned, I owe you big time. By the way, my name is Carlton Elders," he extended his hand to shake mine.

I extended mine and replied, "Nice to meet you . . . again, and under much better circumstances. If you're serious about the offer, I'd be honored to have the opportunity to be part of your team, Mr. Elders."

"Please, call me Carl. All my friends do."

"Very well. Thank you, Carl."

Elders looked down at my application and said, "Your given name, Delbert Bertram Jones, is it? That will never do. I think from now on, we'll just call you Death Bringer or maybe DB for short. How does that sound?"

"Works for me," I said after a bit of hesitation, realizing this was happening. I would take on both the name and persona that had previously only been a fantasy. I was going to become Death Bringer Jones in the flesh. I suddenly felt like an unworthy pretender. I would have to do all I could to make myself worthy of the trust these people were putting in me.

"Look, DB, I know from personal experience, you're more than capable of handling yourself against these deadheads, but I do have to ask, have you ever come up against living Outlanders? You see, as we begin to expand our boundaries outward, not only will we be eradicating any zombies we encounter, but we also experience resistance from renegade Outlanders. As I'm sure you've heard, they can be quite ruthless and violent, and killing a fellow human being is a lot different from taking out something already dead. Not only do they fight back, but from an emotional standpoint, they're still human. Are you ok with killing outlanders as well?"

"That's not going to be a problem for me, Carl," I said. Then I went on to tell him about my last assignment with the army and the encounter with the Outlanders south of Yuengsville.

"Alright then. It sounds like you're exactly what I'm looking for, and I'll tell you what I'm going to do. I'm going to make you a squad commander. You'll oversee a small group of security guards."

I once again was surprised and said, "Thank you for your confidence. It all sounds great to me. But can you explain to me what exactly my squad will be required to do?"

"Here's how I understand things will work," Elders explained, "We'll send out two teams. One team is responsible for clearing brush, installing fencing, and in some cases laying down blacktop. They're our road crew. The other team, your team, will be responsible for protecting them from attack from either the living or the undead. You'll probably also send out scouts to make sure the area ahead is clear as well."

"I've had experiences similar to that in the past in the army," I assured him. "When do we start?"

"Easy there, Death Bringer. We haven't got official approval or funding to start the project yet. It's looking like it will be March or April until we begin sending teams out."

"But that's like five months away. I was hoping for a paying job which would start right away," I said with frustration.

"I understand completely, DB. I think I have a possible solution. I want to bring you on immediately as a paid security consultant. I would fund that position would from a different budget. In that role, you can put together your team, train them, and get them ready when funding for the expansion project is approved. They'll be temporarily paid from the same consulting budget as you, but at a much lower training rate. Once we get the green light, you'll all become direct employees, and you can decide how much of a pay increase each team member will get based on their abilities as you see fit."

I said, "That sounds fair to me. Where will I get my recruits for training? A lot of good people I know are still in the Army and not available."

Elders explained, "I already have a good-sized list of applicants. Many of them, like yourself, have recently been discharged from the Army. One of your first duties will be to go through the list, study their qualifications, and determine which, if any, you might want to interview. Then from that crop, you'll need to pick nine people to hire. We've determined that a ten-person squad is an optimal size; nine plus the squad leader."

"That works for me," I said, "So when do you want me to start?"

"Well, leave me think. It'll probably take me a few days to work out the details. Will next Monday morning be, ok?"

"Sure, that'll work for me," I said. "What time?"

"Whenever you make it in will be ok. We don't worry about stuff like exact time around here. First, it isn't a nine-to-five sort of job. It'll likely be short days at the beginning and much longer days when the expansion begins. Besides, unless you have a wind-up alarm clock, it's sort of hard to make anyone adhere to a schedule without electricity. Whenever you get here, I'll have the list ready for you to start figuring out who you want to interview."

I said, "Thanks again, Carl. I'm looking forward to this."

"And we're looking forward to having the legendary Death Bringer Jones as a squad leader."

He rose to walk me out to the reception area. As we got close, I saw the receptionist, Edna giving me her patented nasty Popeye look. I wondered why Carl put up with such an evil woman but assumed after the apocalypse; pickings were slim. I was just hoping she wouldn't cause me any problems when I started working Monday.

Carl said, "Edna, I'd like to introduce you to our new squad leader, Death Bringer Jones."

Her mouth dropped open as she looked from me to the comic on her desk then back to me again. I swear I saw her go through a dozen different emotions simultaneously. At first, she lost her sour disposition, replaced by one of shock, then disbelief, then what appeared to be awe. A moment later, she seemed to go from surprise to understanding. Eventually, the look she wore was perhaps more disturbing than all the others; she looked at me with total adoration, and dare I say, love, followed by raw lust. I mean to tell you, she looked at me like I was a T-bone steak, and she was a starving junkyard dog. I've had hungry zombies look at me with less desire. I suddenly realized old Edna here would be trouble for sure, but not the sort of trouble I initially thought. She was love-struck.

"D . . .d . . .d . . .d . . . Death Bringer Jones?" She said, continuing to look between me and the comic book, noticing a resemblance she had previously missed. "I . . . I . . . I'm s . . . s . . . so sorry. I . . . I did . . . didn't know!"

If I weren't trying to assume the superhero role, I might have left her stew in her juices for a while longer, but I decided it might be more prudent to take the high road and let her off the hook.

I said, "Not a problem Ma'am. You can never be too careful nowadays. It's good to see you give the security needs of Mr. Elders and this office such a high priority."

That was probably the wrong thing for me to say in her current euphoric state. Her Popeye face suddenly beamed with pride, and I thought I saw a little bit of a girlish blush. I had suddenly gone from being something disgusting you might step in walking on a sidewalk to the most important man in the room.

Carlton said, "Edna can you give me that comic Jack gave you? I want to discuss it with Death Bringer. I'll make sure Jack gets you a new one." The long cigarette ash fell to the floor, and Edna didn't even seem to notice.

She reluctantly handed the comic over, all the while never taking her one open eye off me. Carl said, "And really, Edna, when are you going to quit smoking? I swear someday they're going to be the death of you."

She never took her eyes off me but said, "Well, Mr. Elders, something is surely gonna be the death of me in this new world, so it might as well be something I love."

As we walked away out of earshot, Carl handed me the comic and said, "I was wondering if you could look at this comic, and maybe . . ." He hesitated for a bit then said, "Maybe come up with a uniform or costume if you will, that's somewhat similar to this."

He handed me the comic, and I was surprised to see the so-called costume was not a lot different from the outfit I was thinking about wearing but didn't that day I rescued Carl and his family. The Death Bringer in the comic wore a pair of black leather pants with snakeskin boots. Keep in mind that since the comic was in black and white, I had to make some assumptions regarding the color of his clothing.

Death Bringer appeared to wear a silky black shirt under a black leather vest. On his head, he wore a dark leather cowboy hat with a dark hatband. At the front of the hatband was a shiny, possibly silver belt buckle of a grinning skull with blazing ruby eyes. He wore a dark leather belt with a similar style buckle and the name Death Bringer carved into both sides of the belt itself.

I looked at Carl and said, "Seriously. You want me to dress like this?"

Carl hesitated for a minute, then said, "Well, I suppose yes, as close as you think you can get to this."

"Well, I only have like one pair of leather pants, and I do have a set of snake-skin boots, but I don't have a hat or a belt with buckles like that. I do have a bunch of shirts that should work. I no longer have a vest either."

"Not to worry. I know where I can get you several pairs of black jeans which might be a suitable temporary substitute for the leather pants until we find some more someday. I can also get you a hat and vest like that, and I'm sure I can find a few skull buckles. I know a guy who works with leather who could get me the buckles and would be willing to carve Death Bringer into the leather of the belt as well."

"Well, I suppose if that's what you want, then that's what I'll try to give you," I replied, not confident I was ready to make such a leap. It all sounded good in my imagination, but when I thought about actually walking around town in that outfit, it just seemed a little too corny for me.

"Ok. I can see you're not comfortable with the idea yet, so how about we ease into it. We'll start with jeans and boots and add the hat and belt with buckles later. What do you think?"

I agreed, "Um . . . yeah. I think that might be better."

Carl turned and shook my hand, "Very well then, Death Bringer Jones, we'll see you Monday morning."

CHAPTER 23

NOVEMBER 2043

The following Monday, I found myself sitting at a desk in a cluttered office down the Carlton Elder's office hall. I wore a pair of blue jeans and my snake-skin boots, but that was about as much of the Death Bringer costume as I chose to display at that time, and believe me, that look didn't do a thing to keep Edna from giving me her Popeye love stare every time I walked by. As if it wasn't creepy enough having old Edna looking at me that way, when I imagined the fictional male Popeye cartoon character looking at me like a delicious honey-baked ham, the cringe factor rose to new heights.

Just in case the lusty eyeballing wasn't enough to send chills down my spine, Edna's constant barrage of sexual innuendos certainly did. She would greet me with expressions like, "So this is what a super hunk looks like first thing in the morning. I'd sure love to see how you look right when you step out of bed."

Or she'd say, "What can I do to make you happy, Death Bringer? Just name it, big boy . . . anything!" Then she would wink at me with her one eye that wasn't closed by smoke. I would cringe.

Sometimes she'd make me almost toss my cookies when she'd say, "My, but don't you just look absolutely scrumptious today DB; tastier than a glazed donut."

The truth was, I liked it better when Edna treated me like crap; this lusting after me was more than I could take. I mean, this broad was old enough to be my mother, maybe even my grandmother. What a cougar! Here I was, supposedly some larger-than-life superhero, and I was afraid to walk by Edna's desk because I knew mentally, she was unwrapping me like a lollipop and licking me from head to toe.

Thank goodness this office situation was to be strictly a temporary thing. Once I picked my team and began training them, I'd be out in the field 99% of the time. Speaking of which, I was busy reviewing the applications from potential job candidates when one application stood out for obvious reasons. It was from a recently discharged soldier who had left the Army the same day as me. The name on the application read Alice Janet Hargrove.

It seemed that Alice "Ace" Hargrove got her lesbo butt tossed out of the Army right after me. When I thought about it, it all made perfect sense. Cruz said she needed to get rid of one or two members of her squad that didn't quite fit in. Thinking as Cruz did, she probably figured why not dump two troublemakers simultaneously: me for never quite fitting in and Ace for being a manipulative, deceitful bitch.

I was going to toss her application directly into my round file, then thought better of it. I didn't want to take the chance someone might find it and somehow help make its way back onto my desk. I tore it into four pieces and put the scraps into a leather folder I used to carry papers to and from work. I planned to burn the scraps when I got home, which I did. As far as I was concerned, Ace Hargrove was persona non grata. Good riddance to bad rubbish.

Fortunately, I did find about fifteen other resumes that looked promising. I recognized a few of the names. Some were from my time in the Army or past encounters with them at one time or another. This was the case for both those who I chose to interview and those I decided to eliminate. A few of the ones I dumped immediately were psycho's I remembered from high school, bullies who would have broken my skinny neck if I hadn't been fast enough to outrun them. I was surprised they hadn't fled the town to become Outlanders. At first glance, they seemed more suited for that sort of lifestyle. But then you realize those bully types are cowards at heart and would never survive in the outlands. Still, I figured after surviving getting fragged by Ace Hargrove, the last thing I needed was to have a tribe of lunatics working under me.

After a time, I had to use the men's room but dreaded it, not simply because it was a portable chemical toilet located in an alley outside the office in the November cold. But using it meant I'd have to walk by Edna's desk and endure more of her leering and sexual comments. I didn't want to think about what new and disgusting things she'd come up with if she knew I was coming back from the toilet. My stomach lurched at the thought, but I had no choice. When Mother Nature calls, I must answer.

I quietly made my way down the hall, hoping to sneak by Edna without her noticing. She was sitting at her station, and I could see the bald spot on the back of her head peeking through her cotton candy hair. She appeared to be reading something, probably another Death Bringer comic. If I could just slink past her, I'd be home free. Of course, I'd still have to deal with her innuendos when I returned, but I figured I'd take my small victories wherever I found them. I got behind her and started moving to the right. She was so engrossed in her reading, she never heard me, or so I thought.

As I reached the door and placed my fingers on the handle, I heard a strange sound coming from behind me. It might have been a moan of pleasure or maybe a groan. Whatever it was, the sound was most definitely coming from Edna. I wanted to ignore her and just get outside, but my curiosity got the better of me. I turned and looked back toward her workstation. Edna looked directly at me with an expression that was no longer one of lust but one of hunger as in zombie hunger.

Carl had been right, and Edna's smoking had gotten the better of her. Sometime during that morning, she must have had a heart attack and died at her desk. Now she was back and waiting at the head of the buffet line. The idea of Edna looking at me like fillet mignon had taken on a whole new meaning. She began to get up from her chair, filmed-over eyes staring a hole through me, blackish drool dribbling down her chin. Oddly, the remains of her cigarette still dangled from the right side of her mouth, although at some time, it must have burned out. Her chair fell to the floor with a loud crash.

The thing that had once been Edna began awkwardly staggering toward me, her long boney fingers with their sharp, garishly painted nails reaching out like clawed talons. I knew what I had to do, and although part of me was grateful for the chance to be rid of Edna, I was not thrilled with the idea of taking out an old lady, zombie or not.

As she approached, I heard someone shouting, "Edna! What the hell do you think you're doing?"

I saw Carl had come down the hall from his office as he must have heard the chair falling. The Edna creature turned at the sound of his voice and momentarily lost interest in me. Carl stopped and gaped slack-jawed at the sight of his former receptionist turned zombie. I wished I had come prepared with my katana blades, but I hadn't. I wasn't carrying any weapon at all. I know that sounds ridiculous all things considered, and I should have known better, but at that time, I felt a lot safer inside the fortified walls of the town. After the Edna incident, however, I would never travel anywhere unarmed again, including the bathroom.

So, what to do? What to do? I looked around the room for something to use as a weapon. I assumed old Edna had some scissors in her desk drawer, and if I knocked her down, I could probably get to it. She was so old and scrawny; I could probably just reach over and break her neck. But the thought of touching that now dead, paper-thin skin was disgusting. I had done it dozens of times before, but it was always with zombies I didn't know. The idea of touching an old lady I knew, who in life would have loved having me do so, was far too creepy for me to consider.

I saw two flagpoles in base stands in the corner of the room. One had the Pennsylvania state flag, and the other had the US flag. I didn't know if it was inappropriate to desecrate the state flag, but I did know never to trample on Old Glory. Also, I noticed that the pole holding the state flag had a nasty sharp-looking final at its top, and I knew exactly what to do with it.

Wanting to attract the monster's attention, I ran across the room shouting, "Edna Baby over here!" I was hoping that she might still have a bit of a thing for me somewhere in that moldering brain. Whether she did or not, my shouting was successful in attracting her attention. She turned away from Carl and began lumbering back toward me. I grabbed the flagpole, base, and all and pointed the business end at the creature. Then I charged.

When I made contact, the razor-sharp final on the top of the pole went straight into Edna's throat and out the back of her neck, severing her spinal cord, before my momentum ended up sinking the tip deep into a nearby plaster wall. Dust flew everywhere as the thin drywall collapsed inward. I backed away, letting the heavy base fall to the floor, where it helped to pin the Edna monster in place. She grunted, kicked, and twitched for a moment or so before going still.

A second or two later, I heard a dull thudding sound, and I turned, expecting to see some other undead creature trying to sneak up on me, but instead, I saw Carl slumped over on the hallway floor. I ran to his body, hoping he hadn't had a heart attack and died, or I'd have another zombie to contend with. I know most folks would love the opportunity to put down their bosses, but Carl was ok in my books. Fortunately, he had just passed out and was starting to regain consciousness by the time I reached him.

"Carl? Are you ok?"

"Huh? Um . . . Death Bringer? Thank God you were here!" He said groggily.

"It wasn't a big deal, Carl; she was an old lady. I didn't do anything special."

"No need . . . to be so . . . humble DB. You saved my life, yet again."

I decided to change the subject, and helping him up, I said, "Come on, Carl. Let's get you back to your office. You need to rest for a few minutes and get your sea legs back. Then we have to get someone to get Edna out of here and fix your wall."

"I'll be ok now, thanks to you, Death Bringer."

I decided just to let things go as they were. There was no point in trying to convince Carl that I was anything but superhuman. I had already assumed correctly that this little episode would find its way into one of his son's future comics. I was rapidly becoming a living legend, and I was starting to question if this was all a good idea or not.

CHAPTER 24

DECEMBER 2043

Several weeks had passed since the encounter with Edna, and I was busy interviewing potential candidates for the Systematic Expansion Team. It was early December, and I still had a few candidates to re-interview before I would begin whittling down the original fifteen candidates; I had chosen to just nine, and believe me, this was going to be a daunting task. This challenge was all new to me. I was usually the person rejected, not the guy doing the choosing.

All the candidates had something I felt the team needed, but I knew six of them wouldn't make the cut. I was also concerned that even though they all looked good on paper, maybe when we began training, some of them that I thought would be perfect might not be. I had an idea I wanted to speak to Carl about to see if he thought it was feasible. As luck would have it, moments later, he came into my office.

"How goes the hunt, Death Bringer?" He asked.

It was amazing how I had gotten used to people referring to me by that name in just a month or so. It was like I was born to carry that handle. I know that sounds goofy, but that's how I felt. I decided now was the time to bring up my idea.

"It's tough to choose, to be honest with you."

"Yes, I'm sure it is. I looked over the fifteen applications you chose, and I'm sure even after interviewing them, the decision to select just nine is tough."

"Here is my concern, Carl. If I choose what I think are my top nine candidates, then I'll likely lose the others as they find other places to work. Then suppose when I start the training process, I discover that two or three of my chosen nine can't cut it? Then I either must go with a smaller squad or offer opportunities to six I turned down, hoping they're still interested, or start the process all over again to try to find others to fill the slots."

"Well, I suppose that could very well happen. It's not uncommon in situations like this, I'm sure. But I suspect you have an alternate suggestion for me to consider. Am I right?"

I smiled and said, "You most certainly are. I was thinking of bringing on all fifteen applicants at a training pay rate, with the understanding that it was a trial run only. When we finished, there would only be nine remaining that would make up the team. This way, only the best would remain. Some might quit. Some might not be up to my standards, and some might get hurt during training or, God forbid, killed. We'd make it clear that this is a type of competition where the best nine would be the team, and the rest would go home."

"Hum . . . yes. I think I like that. This way, we would be guaranteed to have a full team and get the best of the best. At the start of training, we could also point out that this is only the first of potentially several teams we will be putting together; we'll call it Alpha Team. Eventually, I hope to have more than four separate teams dedicated to expanding our perimeters in all directions. If they don't make the Alpha Team, perhaps later they could try out for one of the others. Also, we're not the only fortified town that will be participating in Systematic Expansion. We're probably one of the smallest towns. Yuengsville will be putting together many more teams than we will. Perhaps they would have better luck at one of the other towns or cities."

"What about the money for the additional six trainees. Can you swing that?" I asked.

Carl said, "Not to worry, DB. I'll find the money for training somewhere. This process is far too important not to do things the right way. So, when do you think you can start training our recruits?"

"I think I should be ready in a week or so. I must notify the fifteen candidates and give them a start date. Then I have to finish putting together a training program for them."

"How is the training program going?" Carl asked.

I said, "I'm progressing nicely. We'll start out doing things inside since it's getting so cold outside. I found a place that I think will work well for this. You know the building that used to house Chick's Catering service?"

"Yes, I recall it."

"Well, right now, it's still abandoned, and it has a nice size room where he used to hold banquets, and that room has a wood fireplace in it. I figure we can use that space like a gym for exercise and weapons training."

"Great idea," Carl said, "I'll make sure the town council knows to reserve that building for you."

"Now here's where things get a bit trickier," I explained, "On warmer days, I plan on taking the team outside the walls, into the outlands, probably toward the end of their training. Also, when I feel they're up to the challenge, I want to have them experience actual encounters with the undead. If they're going to be part of the team, they have to know how to kill zombies. A few of them have prior experience, but not all of them do."

Carl thought for a moment, then said, "It's too bad we can't figure out a way to give them that same exposure here inside the town."

"Are you suggesting rounding up dead heads and bringing them inside? Hell, capturing them is more dangerous than killing them," I said, surprised.

"Yeah, you're probably right about that. But I tell you what we could do. We could build a sort of corral near one of our borders with an opening to the outlands. Then whenever a zombie found its way into the cage, we could shut the outer gate trapping it inside. That way, when you were ready, you could bring your trainees into the corral and teach them how to deal with the creatures."

"Yes. I think I like that idea, but here's what I would recommend," I said. "I think we should build the corral as you suggested but have like four or five fenced-in cattle shoots leading from the outer barrier to the corral. This way, we could allow the shoots to fill up with dead heads and control how many we want to allow into the corral at a time. It would also give us a good supply of zombies for future training sessions without delaying our progress."

Carl said, "Yes. I like that a lot. I know your plate is full right now, but if you could put together a rough sketch of what you have in mind with some approximate dimensions, I could have my road crew find a location and start building it right away. They could use the practice since they'll be the crew you'll eventually be protecting when the expansion starts in earnest."

"Great idea," I said, "As far as a location, it would be convenient if the corral went behind Chick's Catering. That place is near one of our barriers which would make it a perfect location. As far as a design is concerned, I'll get on it as soon as I send out the notices for training to start. So how about two weeks from now? Will that be enough time?"

Carl said, "Yeah. That'll work. I'm glad to see this is all coming together."

"Me too," I replied.

CHAPTER 25

JANUARY 2044

I stood in the center of my makeshift training center in the former Chick's Catering building with a blazing fire roaring in the fireplace, heating the ample space while outside a storm raged blanketing the town with more than eight inches of snow. I looked around the area at the fifteen candidates. They had trudged through the winter storm for the sole purpose of taking their shot at being part of my squad.

"My squad." That sounded so strange to me. I began feeling overwhelmed as that all too familiar sense of inadequacy once again began to rear its ugly head. I began to wonder. Who was I? I was no one, an imposter, a pretender, a fraud. What right did I have to command these fine men and women? Hell, I had been tossed out of the Army a few months ago. Who was Death Bringer Jones anyway? Wasn't he nothing more than a work of fiction, some teenage boy's comic book hero?

I tried to stand tall in front of my trainees although I wanted to turn and run. To make matters worse, I was in full Death Bringer costume, which did little to help improve my level of discomfort. Carl had gotten me both the black leather cowboy hat with the silver skull buckle and a matching belt and buckle. Also, the name "Death Bringer" was carved elegantly on both sides of the belt. I had the black leather vest over a dark shirt as well. Here I was, right out of the comic book, the legendary Death Bringer Jones. Sadly, I felt a lot more like Delbert Bertram, super nerd at that moment.

Then I realized this was a pivotal moment in my life. No matter how strange or inadequate I might feel, I had to make these recruits believe I was the same hero they had seen in the comics. But to make them believe in me, I had to believe in myself. I had to either become Death Bringer or forget the whole thing. I had to either go big or go home.

I looked over to my right and saw Carl walking out onto the floor to introduce me to the group. Yes, I had met them and interviewed them individually, but now I was being cast in the role of their leader. I wasn't just their leader, but I was the living, breathing personification of the comic book Death Bringer Jones.

Back when I initially interviewed each of them, they knew me only as Mr. Jones. I made a point of not mentioning anything about Death Bringer. Now I stood before them in full zombie slayer costume. I watched them watching me with a variety of expressions. Some were astonished, some were happy, and a few looked at me as if I had just appeared from some sort of interstellar portal and was a strange being never before seen in this universe.

I understood I was going to have to force myself into the role of Death Bringer Jones entirely so that not a single speck of doubt would manage to sneak through my facade. I kept repeating inside my mind, "You are Death Bringer. You are Death Bringer. You are Death Bringer."

I heard Carl speaking from what seemed like a million miles away until I could come back to earth and focus on what he said.

"Ladies and Gentlemen. I want to congratulate you, fifteen talented individuals, for making it this far in the process. Being considered for a place on the Systematic Expansion Security Team Alpha is an honor. You will be the pioneers in this exercise, and your performance will determine whether this program succeeds or fails. However, as you are all aware, being chosen for this training was not the final phase in the process. Unfortunately, we will only be able to select nine of you to hire as actual members of the Alpha Team. The rest will have to try for one of the other teams. We will make the decision over the next two months, and believe me, these eight weeks will be some of the toughest weeks you have ever endured."

I listened but disagreed with what Carl was saying. He was speaking like a manager or a politician, not someone who understood military training. I knew that several of the applicants had been members of the various branches of the armed forces before the apocalypse, and as such,

had survived boot camp along with lots of other types of intense training. Some were combat veterans who would not be impressed by flowery
speeches from some suit or so-called leaders dressed like some comic
book hero. Any one of them was more qualified to lead this squad than I
was. But it was my responsibility, and I had every intention of doing the
job to the best of my abilities.

Carl continued, "As part of the SE Alpha Team, you will be playing
a significant role not only in helping our little community, but you will
be part of a network of other SE members. You will all be working to
make our entire country a more robust, better, and safer place to live. Do
not be mistaken people, we are at war here, and the enemy is among the
living and the dead. There are still millions of undead creatures roaming
throughout the outlands. These towns, cities, and safe zones are nothing
more than small islands of protection amid a vast sea of zombies and
criminals.

"The next few years will likely go down in the history books as the
time of the Zombie Wars; a war to save humanity from the undead. The
history books will probably skim over, as most historical accounts always
have in the past; we are also at war with our fellow man. By that, I mean
the Outlanders. History will speak of what we will do to eradicate the
dead but say little about the living enemy. That particular chore is not a
tasteful responsibility, but still one we must carry out.

"Keep in mind these renegades are ruthless killers, and although
their numbers may be fewer than those of the undead, their threat to us
is much more significant. These criminals are living, breathing humans
who have skills and working brains like the rest of us. When they attack,
it's with knives, spears, and yes, guns and explosives. They will lurk in
the outlands waiting for us. Their style of warfare will be of the guerilla
variety. They will hide in the woods, up in the trees, in caves in tunnels,
anywhere they can, to gain the element of surprise. They'll set traps, use
IEDs, whatever it takes to try to kill you, and your charges to prevent us
from expanding out into what they see as their territory.

"They may use snipers to try to pick off our workers one by one. It
will be your job to make sure that doesn't happen. During the next two
months, you will all be trained in various forms of combat so that you

will be able to venture out into the savage outlands and keep our workers safe while destroying any enemy forces who try to stand in our way.

"As you may have noticed, there is no press her at this time. This lack of media is because what we must tell you is not going to be for publication. Each of you has signed a nondisclosure form, so whether you are chosen to be part of the team or not, you cannot divulge anything you hear, learn, or do during your training sessions. I will meet with the press outside as soon as I'm finished here. Now I suppose I've droned on long enough. So, without further ado, I would like to officially introduce you to your squad leader and training instructor. Ladies, and gentlemen, I give you Death Bringer Jones."

I heard various reactions from the crowd, most of which were sounds of shock, surprise, and realization. These trainees just figured out why I dressed the way I did and who I was. I took two apprehensive steps forward as Carl began clapping, signaling to the trainees that it was ok for them to do likewise. Soon the room erupted in applause. Carl turned, waved goodbye to the trainees, and headed out the door to meet the press.

Raising my hand, I signaled for the applause to stop, which it eventually did. I looked at my fifteen recruits making sure to make silent eye contact with each one of them. I waited until I heard the door to the outside close amid the storm of reporters' questions. I turned, and faced my trainees, and said, "Hello again, people, and welcome. I want to make a few things clear from the start. No matter what you may have heard about me or read in the various comics circulating throughout town, I am no superhero. I'm just a regular human being, just like the rest of you. I may excel in a few areas but so do each of you. We are here to become a team. Although each of us may have individual strengths, the combined total of our talents can be greater than the sum of those individual strengths.

"Mr. Elders said this could be the most challenging training you will ever experience. I beg to differ. I've read your files. I know what you've been through before coming here. You have all endured some severe hardships, as have I. This training will not be like any you've ever had in that it will be more rewarding. I can't know everything you all know; it simply isn't possible. Some of you have skills I've never encountered.

But we can work together and teach each other. My approach will be a bit unorthodox, but I believe it will work. Although I've been designated squad leader and training coordinator, each one of us here will, at one time or another will assume a training role as we share our knowledge, experience, and skills with each other.

"Oh yeah, and this costume. It was Mr. Elder's idea. His son is the one who came up with the comic. It's for the press, for the public. He thinks it will help promote the program. I don't mind wearing it if that's what it takes to make this all a success. But I should point out; I'm not assuming the role of some kid's imaginary character. This fictional Death Bringer was born after I saved Mr. Elders, his son, his wife, and two others from a mob of zombies a few days after all this crap started. A woman I had previously saved came up with the name Death Bringer. The comic came later. I thought it was important you all know the difference; now on to business."

I had taken the time to memorize the names and faces of each of the applicants during their interviews. I looked at a large muscular young man and said, "Jim Holman. You're a former marine, skilled in hand-to-hand combat, and have black belts in several different martial arts styles. Is that correct?"

"Sir, that is correct, Sir," he replied, snapping to attention.

"At ease, Jim. We are all team members here. You can just call me D.B. Is that ok with you?"

"That . . . that's fine with me, Sir, I mean D.B.," he said with obvious discomfort.

"Your skills will help those who have little such experience, thereby making the team stronger. Sarah Michigan. Before this opportunity, you worked as a physician's assistant. You're a well-educated young woman whose first aid knowledge will be extremely valuable to our team."

A young, attractive woman of average height and build replied, "I'd be happy to share everything I know with the team . . . D.B."

Then I said, "And Sam Dawson, you were a demolitions expert in the army. I can hardly believe they let you leave with all that knowledge."

"I agree," he said, smiling. Then with a smirk, he said, "Then again, they let you leave, didn't they?"

Nervous chuckles spread throughout the crowd. It was public knowledge that I had once been in the army and had they had let me go as well. I realized it might be time for a change in the direction of the conversation.

"Point taken," I replied. "Anyway, what I'm trying to express here is that each one of us has something to contribute, and all of us have something to learn from each other. Unfortunately, we all can't learn everything. There is neither the time nor the desire nor the skill level for such an undertaking. My job is to ensure I have properly used these various skills when the Systematic Expansion Program begins. Now I think I've said enough for the time being. Keep in mind; this entire situation is fluid, ever-evolving, and subject to change at any time. Are there any questions?"

The group remained silent, looking back, and forth waiting to see who would address the one point that was most important to them all. A young man raised his hand and said, "I have a question . . . D.B."

It was a recruit by the name of Bill Jenkins. He was an older man who I recalled was somewhere about thirty-five or thirty-six. He had been conscripted into the army around the same time I had, and he was part of the caravan Deimos had attacked. That group of outlaw renegades allowed the zombies to get at our crew. At first, I thought he might comment about Outlanders, but instead, he addressed the obvious.

"I have a concern about the fact that there are fifteen of us here, and only nine will make the final cut. If it's true that we all have something to contribute and something to gain from each other, then why will only nine of us be chosen?"

I took a deep breath and said, "That's a good question, Bill, and one I'm sure is on everyone's mind. One thing that was true before the apocalypse and has not changed since is that money talks. The short and sweet answer is budget constraints. First, let me say that although I doubt this will happen, it is still possible that after we complete our training, funding for the Systematic Expansion Project might not even happen, and we could all be sent home. It's also possible that funding will be less than desired, and we might only have money for five or six of you. Likewise, it's always possible that more money than we thought might be available, and all fifteen of you might be able to participate. Then again, just because you might not be part of the Alpha Team, going through the training program will automatically put you at the top of the list for Beta Team or any of the other teams which may follow. Plus, as Mr. Elders mentioned, lots of the other fortified cities will be forming their own SE teams, so you very well could become part of one of those teams. The point here is that each of you should do your best to learn as much as possible; it can only help you down the road."

I looked around the room and saw a variety of emotions pass over their faces. Some of them looked happy with what I had said. Some looked concerned, and others seemed very skeptical to suggest I was shoveling a bunch of crap at them. Well, there was little I could do about that other than show them I was serious about this team.

I asked, "Are there any other questions?"

The room was silent.

"Alright then," I said, "Let's get this show on the road."

CHAPTER 26

MARCH 2044

For the record, I did consider going into great detail about the training process and all the things I went through as part of this story, but then I became concerned it might all be painfully dull. I mean, I thought the whole thing was cool and exciting, but looking at it as a reader rather than the writer, I realized it could turn into a major snooze fest.

So instead, I decided to touch on one or two significant events during our training, which I thought you might find interesting. Then I'll wrap it all up and tell you how things ended. Sound like a plan? Yeah, I thought it might.

The first situation occurred when we decided to pit each applicant against a pair of zombies. Keep in mind this was after weeks of rigorous training in hand-to-hand combat, as well as weapons training. In this exercise, the challenger was not permitted to have any firearms and could only have one knife and one blunt club of their choosing.

This challenge took place inside the corral; Carl's men had done a fantastic job with my design. A ten-foot-high fence topped with razor wire surrounded the open area. This safety precaution assured none of the undead could get out. A single wire gate allowed us access to the corral. Along the back, near the outer perimeter of the town, five separate wire fence tunnels stretched beyond the protective barrier. I designed these not as open-top cattle chutes but tunnels to guarantee any zombies wandering inside would remain as intact as possible. Now that concept might sound a bit strange but allow me to explain.

During my scouting in the outlands, I learned that whenever zombies became stationary for too long, they tended to attract flocks of turkey vultures and other woodland creatures that fed on carrion. The last thing I needed was nature's garbage crew making off with my training tools. We did have to fire rifles into the air to scare off the flocks of hundreds of predators from time to time. We also had to put rat traps around the tunnels to keep vermin from coming in and gnawing on the merchandise.

As long as the deadheads were moving, most of the creatures steered clear, but I was still glad I had designed the tunnels, so the dead ones remained as viable as possible. The cold weather managed to keep the flies at bay for the most part, but spring was looming on the horizon, so I had to make sure I got this portion of the exercise over before the thaw. If another team were ready to use the corral in the spring, that would be their problem.

Anyway, each potential team member had a chance in the arena, and each did a fantastic job. I stood by with my katana blades in case anything went wrong. Unfortunately, I should have had a guard standing by with a gun as well. In fact, since that day in the corral, it has become standard protocol to have a team of two snipers on hand during any actual zombie-based training exercises. We had formerly called "zombie-based" exercises "live zombie" the exercises, but "live zombie" seemed like too much of an oxymoron.

As things worked out, our final applicant to enter the ring was Sarah Michigan, the woman with the medical training I had mentioned earlier. I wanted her on my team as medically trained people were hard to find. I couldn't understand why she even wanted to be part of Alpha Team. She could have easily made much more money working at the local medical center. However, she insisted she wanted to be part of the squad.

During our initial interview, she had told me, "People will be getting hurt on this team. Workers clearing brushes with gas-powered tools will be injured, and those building fences and using hand tools. These potential injuries don't even consider Alpha Team's security squad. Skirmishes with zombies, and especially encounters with Outlanders, will require medical support. But I want to be more than the person who patches up injuries. I want to be one of the team members who slays zombies and defends against Outlanders."

I had asked her, "What about your oath to 'do no harm'?" How can you justify being a fighter after that?"

She had smiled and said, "I swore to 'do no harm' medically, and I won't. If we injured and captured any Outlanders, my sworn duty would be to provide medical assistance to the prisoners. But in the heat of battle, I plan to inflict as much harm as possible. Remember, I know where on the body to hit to make my attacks fatal; no repair work required."

Sarah entered the corral as I shut the gate behind her. She held a long-bladed knife in her right hand and a length of thick wire covered with rubber in the other. The wire was about 18 inches long and about an inch in diameter. Inside the thick black rubber casing were more than a dozen interlaced strands of heavyweight aluminum wire. I had some prior experience with such a weapon. It was both flexible, painful, and a highly effective skull cracker in the right hands. I believed Sarah had those hands.

I signaled to the guard manning the tunnels to release one zombie from each of the two cages. An average-sized male and skeletal-thin female shuffled into the arena, and Sarah didn't waste a second. She charged at the female, swinging her war club and slamming it so hard into the side of the thing's skull that the creature's neck broke instantly, and its head cracked open as it hit the ground, spilling its gray matter onto the dirt amid a spreading pool of puss.

Before the first zombie hit the ground, Sarah was already shoving the blade of her knife into the throat of the male zombie, where she twisted it with a loud audible crack, severing the thing's spinal column. The zombie fell to the ground as Sarah, never letting go of the knife's handle, pulled it free with a disgusting, sucking sound. The crowd of trainees went wild, recognizing the time it took Sarah to take down her zombies was a fraction of that of the rest of the team.

Amid the cheers and applause, someone was screaming from the outer perimeter of the corral. The voice cried, "Look out, look out, the gates are open. Sarah turned to find two of the gates to the tunnels standing wide open, sending almost a dozen zombies into the corral with her. I grabbed the entrance gate, slipped inside, and pulled it tightly closed behind me. Some of my trainees had made it to the gate and tried to open it to help us.

"Stay out there!" I shouted, "I got this. I'll just be a minute."

I turned and ran headlong at the zombies, freeing my two katana blades as I did. I passed Sarah as she had taken a defensive posture, waiting for the creatures to get close enough to fight. I felt confident if any of the monsters got past me, Sarah would clean them up. Everything happened so quickly; I can scarcely recall most of it. All I know is I went into the crowd of undead monsters swinging my blades, one in each hand amid a flurry of blood and body parts. I jumped, I twisted, I turned, I spun in circles, I even danced a bit, all the while relieving the creatures of their limbs.

When I finished, I stood panting, my breaths coming in ragged catches, sweat running down my face, despite the cold temperatures. Bits of zombie flesh, brains, and blood covered me from head to toe. My ears rang with the sounds of my own whoops, and war cries. Then I heard more than a dozen voices calling, "Death Bringer! Death Bringer!" Everyone was screaming and cheering. I looked down at my feet and saw I was standing in a sea of severed heads and limbs as gallons of zombie gore seeped downward, soaking into the dirt floor of the corral. I turned, and stepping over corpse parts, I pushed the two open gates closed and locked them.

I walked over to see how Sarah was, and she ran up to me, hugging me and shouting, "Oh my God! I swear, I've never seen anything like that in my life. You . . . you were amazing! You truly are Death Bringer Jones."

"Twern't nothin' Ma'am," I said with a smile. Then I noticed the clapping and shouting had stopped, and when I turned to look, I saw all my trainees staring at me with nothing short of astonishment. I said, "We're supposed to be zombie slayers, aren't we? Well, that's how we do it uptown."

One by one, they came to me, eyes wide with astonishment. Every one of them was ogling me like I was a movie star or someone special like that. I wouldn't have been surprised if they asked me for my autograph. It was bizarre since I had hand-picked this team and trained with them for almost two months. We had become like a family, yet now all of a sudden, I was some sort of untouchable superhero.

CHAPTER 27

The second event I wanted to record happened a week later. I was taking the entire team outside the perimeter of the town into the outlands. They had proven their abilities against the undead, at least in a controlled situation, but I needed to test them in a real-world mission. Our assignment was to simulate a scenario where we would be protecting a Systematic Expansion road crew as they cleared and marked an area for future barrier construction.

Since we were still awaiting funding approval, there was no money for actual barrier construction. But we could at least go through the exercise and marked the cleared areas. We knew once funds were available, we'd have to clear the place all over again, but this was still an excellent opportunity for the team to prove they could work well together, not only security team members but road crew as well. If everything went according to plan, we might encounter a few deadheads, take them out then come home. But who said anything ever goes according to plan?

Carl had arranged for a group of about six of his maintenance men who were to eventually be assigned to the road crew to drive a convoy of two trucks to the woods outside the city's perimeter. We walked in front and alongside the vehicles until we reached the edge of the woods. We were no more than three hundred feet or more from the edge of the city barriers. The road crew exited their trucks and began hammering four-foot-high stakes into the ground. Their purpose was to string wire from the stakes back to the town wall to represent the expansion border. The first pole was no more than a few inches in the ground when I heard one of the crew screaming, "Oh my God, here they come."

Before we had a chance to think, several dozen zombies came lurching out of the woods heading straight for us. Typically, the guards at the gates would pick off these creatures. But with all of us out there in the line of fire, the ball was in our court. The responsibility fell on us to take care of these monsters. The road crew supervisor followed protocol and ordered all workers back into the trucks, where they rolled up the windows, started their engines, and waited for my team to do what they trained to do, which we did.

Each member of my crew took the weapon of their choice and went to work. Although we carried firearms, we agreed not to use them for this exercise; no guns would unless necessary. The reason for this was because of our proximity to each other. I didn't want to risk someone accidentally hit by friendly fire. But if things got dangerous or ugly, we were prepared, and ugly was imminent by the looks of what was coming our way.

Spears, knives, swords, axes, clubs, and homemade weapons without names began making quick work of the approaching hoard. My Katana blades took down zombie after zombie. I ordered my team to spread out and form a semi-circle around the convoy of trucks; this was a maneuver I had taught them during training. It served two purposes. It created a border that prevented the creatures from getting at the workers, and it also gave the work crew an opening in case things went south and they needed to retreat backward.

I looked over and saw Jake McGuire swinging some sort of ax/spear combination weapon he had made himself. It was about seven feet long with a razor-sharp tip and a double-sided ax blade that could and did remove heads at an alarming rate. In between decapitations, Jake used the spear tip to gouge eye sockets, jab throats, and do whatever was necessary to take down the monsters. I thought to myself, not only was Jake a shoo-in to make my team, but I felt he had what it took to be the leader of his squad someday. Who knows, maybe eventually he'd get the opportunity.

Not far from Jake, a young female recruit named Connie Newsom was having a lot of trouble, which didn't surprise me. She was someone I was unsure of since the beginning when I interviewed her. However, she seemed to have all the necessary credentials to do the job, at least on paper, something about her when we did the face-to-face interview set off some of my internal alarms. Unfortunately, since humanity was just barely starting to creep back from the edge of near extinction, it was virtually impossible to verify much of what appeared on the applications. That was the purpose of our training time. It was supposed to give me a chance to weed out anyone who might have lied on their applications. But so far, Connie had managed to hold her own. She had the slowest time during the zombie exercise in the corral, but I had just attributed that to maybe having an off day. But now, I could see I was wrong to doubt my initial suspicions.

She was in full panic mode. She had dropped her weapon of choice, a sword, and was standing unarmed, frozen with fright, and practically catatonic. Jake had just finished off the last of his zombies and ran over to save her. Likewise, Bill Jenkins was coming to her aid from the other direction. I focused on filling in the hole left by Jake as he and Bill quickly dispatched the approaching deadheads. Connie had made my decision of which team member to cut first an easy one.

When the last of the zombies were down, I shouted. "Ok, everyone, I think that's more than enough for today's exercise. Let's head back."

But no sooner had the words left my mouth when I heard the crack of gunfire. Then I saw one of my recruits lose the top of his skull in a shower of brains and blood.

I screamed, "Sniper!" and pointed to the area of the forest where I had seen a flash of light. All my remaining team members drew their weapons, turned, and pumped round after round into the wooded area I had pointed. After a few seconds, an unearthly silence fell over our world. I could smell the stench of the slaughtered undead, along with the smell of sweat, gun smoke, and fear.

I shouted, "Sarah, follow me! Holman and McGuire stay with the trucks. The rest of you go into the woods, make sure nothing is still living out there, then report back here as soon as possible."

I ran to see which of my trainees had been shot. I had asked Sarah to follow me if there was still time to save him, but I knew it was a moot point. When we arrived at the body, we saw it was a young man named Joe Jenson. He wasn't much older than I was, maybe about twenty-three, but that was as old as he was ever going to get. The young man lay on his back in the dirt. The top of his head was gone. His brain was nothing more than a mass of gray mush soaking into the earth.

Turning to Sarah, I said, "He's beyond our help now. Sorry, Sarah."

Tears streamed down her cheeks as she looked helplessly down at her dead comrade. I was now down from fifteen trainees to thirteen. Little did I know that by the end of the day, Sarah would announce she was leaving the team, and my list would fall to twelve candidates; not that it would matter anyway.

McGuire helped me load Jensen's body into the back of the truck. Then I turned and saw the rest of my team coming back from the woods. Four of them were dragging two bodies behind them by the legs. When they reached us, I went over to examine the corpses. Both of them were dead, and both were human Outlanders. The first one's body was riddled with bullets from head to toe. He was damaged so badly it was hard not to mistake him for a zombie. Fortunately, more shots than I cared to count found their way into his skull, so this one was going to stay dead.

The second one had minor bullet damage, but his arms and legs twisted into shapes no human body should form. I noticed a crudely rendered tattoo on his mangled arm. It was a capital letter D drawn in red ink, appearing to drip blood. I recognized it as the mark of that lunatic Deimos.

"I think this one was your sniper," one of the recruits said, "See how his body looks like it took a lot fewer bullets compared to the other guy. It looks to me like he was hit and fell from a tree. That's when his arms and legs got all busted up."

"Was his neck broken, or was he shot in the head?" I asked, studying the body carefully. That was when I saw his right hand twitch. He opened his eyes coated with the film of death, and a deep growl erupted from deep in his throat. Then his mouth began opening and closing rhythmically as his lips curled back in a snarl, revealing his yellowed and rotted teeth.

I stepped back the brought both blades down simultaneously on the top of his head, slicing his skull into thirds. He fell back to the ground, dead for the last time. I looked at the trainees and said, "Leave these scum bags here to rot. Let's go home now."

CHAPTER 28

There were no more incidents that day as we made our way back through the town gates and into our training building. We brought Jensen's body inside and laid him on the floor covered in a blanket. I would have to tell Carl about everything that happened, and believe me; I wasn't looking forward to that conversation. Carl trusted me to be the leader he thought I could be, but I had failed him. Maybe Cruz was right. Maybe all I was good for was going off on my own, being a lone wolf. No matter how hard I tried, I suppose I wasn't meant to play well with others.

The proof of this was the corpse lying on the floor under the bloody blanket. Between Jensen's death and Connie freezing up, the exercise had been a complete catastrophe. If Carl told me to hit the bricks, he would be more than justified. At that moment, I thought things couldn't get much worse. Then Sarah came up to me with a look of incredible sadness on her face.

"Hey, Sarah," I said, "How are you holding up?"

"Not good," she said, then broke down crying, "Oh D.B. I . . . I thought I could do this. I thought I had what it took to be part of Alpha Team, but I was so, so wrong."

"Look, Sarah, today was tough for everyone, including me. Losing Jensen was a tragedy."

She sniffed, then said, "Yes, of course, it was. But this is what life on Alpha Team will always be. Every time we go out, there's a chance one or more of us won't make it back."

I said, "That's very true, Sarah. But I thought you realized that from the start."

"I thought I did too. But I was wrong."

"Sarah, when Carl explained way back on that first day of training that we were at war, he wasn't exaggerating. We are at war with the undead, and we are greatly outnumbered. We are at war with the Outlanders. Although their numbers are few, they are savage killers. Most of them are probably insane. They've been living like animals for almost a year. They live out there in the outlands among the undead and still managing to survive. It takes a special sort of madness to pull that off."

"I know that D.B. But today showed me that I don't have what it takes to do what your team will have to do day after day. You were right to question my motivation during my interview. I thought I could do this, but I was wrong. I'm not a killer; I'm a doctor, a healer. I'm taking myself out of the running and going back to my real calling, medicine. I'm so sorry, D.B., but I've made up my mind."

I wasn't sure what to say. So simply nodded and said nothing. Sarah turned and walked away to join her fellow team members across the floor as far from Jensen's body as possible. I wasn't surprised she had quit. I saw her face out there in the heat of battle, and although Sarah hadn't frozen as Connie had, I could tell she was done. I think I probably knew she would quit even before she did.

Word of our troubles must have spread through the town like a wildfire because, within a few minutes, Carlton Elders came rushing into the building. He held a stack of envelopes in his hand, which I found strange since payday was two days away. He came up to me and looked down at the covered body on the floor. Blood was sleeping through the blanket.

"Oh no. So, what I heard was true," Carl said.

"Yes," that was all I could manage to say.

"It's just so tragic."

He asked, "Any other casualties?"

I said, "No others killed or wounded. But Connie Newsom froze up out there and could have endangered the squad with her inaction. I'll be notifying her that she's off the squad as soon as possible."

"Agreed," he said. I couldn't help but feel like something else was going on with Carl I didn't know about. He seemed a bit off to me. Maybe it was just the fact that things had turned out so badly with our first trip into the outlands. Perhaps it was something else. Whatever it might be, I suspected I would find out shortly.

I took a deep breath and said, "There's more, Carl. Sarah Michigan is resigning and pulling herself out of the competition. Today was just too much for her."

"Well," Carl replied, "It's probably for the best."

Once again, I got that strange vibe from Carl. It was like he was standing there, but his mind was a million miles away.

"I had high hopes for Sarah," I said, looking down at Jensen's covered body, and asked, "I forget Carl. Did Joe Jensen have any living relatives? Is there someone a next of kin to notify?"

Carl returned to earth and said, "No. No one. His family died in the first week of the apocalypse. He was all alone. I suspect that's what drew him to us. We might be a dysfunctional bunch, but we were all the family he had."

"I suppose there are more of us in his situation than we realize, Carl. You're fortunate to have your wife and your son."

"Don't I know that! But I'll never forget that the only reason I still have them at all is that you saved us. Had you not showed up that day, one or all of us would be gone, D. B."

"I told you to forget about that, Carl. You know there's no need for you to make a big deal out of that. Anyone would have done the same, and besides, you guys took up the fight and did an amazing job that day."

He looked at me as a sudden sadness crossed his face and said, "Say what you will, D. B., but you saved us all that day, which makes what I have to tell you that much more impossible to say."

I realized that those strange vibrations I was feeling coming off Carl were not my imagination, but we're accurate. Something was wrong, and like it or not, I was about to find out about it.

"What, what are you saying, Carl? What exactly do you have to tell me?"

"I have some bad news for you and the team.

CHAPTER 29

I stared at Carl, unsure I was ready to hear his bad news, not after the day I had already experienced. What could be worse than a dead trainee? But then I understood what he was going to tell me a second before he spoke.

"I'm sorry, D.B., but I just found out ten minutes ago that the proposed funding for the Systematic Expansion Project has been drastically cut."

"Cut? You mean cut as in we have to reduce the size of our team?"

He hesitated for an uncomfortable moment of silence, then said, "No. Cut as in there will be no Systematic Expansion Program for our town and many other small towns for some time to come; perhaps as long as a decade."

"What do you mean?"

"Here's what they told me. The newly formed national government jumped the gun on the SE program, especially while planning to start that undead program's bounty. That one has some fancy government number DK something or other, but I can't remember what the hell it is. Some news guy jumped on the initials DK and has dubbed it the Dead Kill program. You know, killing something already dead. The government has determined they don't have sufficient funds to take on both massive programs simultaneously. Also, as you've unfortunately learned today, the problems in the outlands are many. Not only with the undead but the Outlanders themselves. It's a greater problem than the government realized."

I asked, "So what do they plan to do about it?"

Carl said, "They plan to get the Dead Kill program started immediately, which will essentially kick off the zombie wars. They may start the SE program in larger cities nationwide and in Pennsylvania with cities like Philadelphia and Pittsburgh. After a few years, when the population of the undead dwindles, then the SE program will start up in smaller cities then eventually in towns our size."

"So, what does that mean for these folks?" Indicating my team members, who were at the far end of the building, sitting and occasionally looking over in our direction. I suspected they were less concerned with Carl and me and more concerned with their dead teammate lying beneath the bloody blanket.

Carl said, "In a few minutes, I'll go over there and break the news to them. They'll return home immediately, as will you, Death Bringer. I have all your money here in these envelopes. Again, I'm so sorry, D. B., especially since I think your team would have been one of the best."

"I understand, Carl," I said, although the truth was, I didn't. I never understood the workings of politicians. But what else could I say? Much like on the night the dead began to rise, my job no longer existed. Then I asked him, "Carl. I appreciate you wanting to fire the team personally, but if you don't mind, it's something I should do myself."

"Yeah. You're probably right about that. Would you mind I tagged along in case there are some questions you might not have answers for?"

I agreed, "That's probably a good idea. Besides, you have the team's pay."

"There is that," he said.

We walked over to the group, and as we approached, I could see looks of apprehension on all of their faces. I suspected they worried they were about to get chewed out for the fiasco, which our first mission had become. Unfortunately, what I was about to tell them would be much worse. I looked at Connie Newsom, who knew she had blown it out there. At least I wouldn't have to single her out and cut her from the team. I suppose that was one ray of sunshine in this fecal downpour.

"Ok, everyone," I said, "Listen up. We have an unfortunate announcement to make." The trainees looked back and forth between each other, obviously unsure of what was coming. I continued, "Look. There's no delicate way to do this, so since we're all in this together, I think it's best if I just tear off the Band-Aid in one hard tug. The Systematic Expansion Program has been indefinitely suspended. Alpha team has been disbanded as of right now."

I waited for a few seconds to let that all sink in. Everyone sat in stunned silence.

"Mr. Elders has envelopes for each of us—yes, I'm out of a job too—, and I'll hand them out as soon as we're finished. We'll all be paid up to the end of the day today. Isn't that right, Mr. Elders?"

Carl flinched at the mention of his name, then regained his composure. I'm sure he felt highly uncomfortable standing in front of this group of hardened trainees and having to be the bearer of such bad news. "Yes . . . yes, that's correct. In addition, I've provided a letter of recommendation for each of you. It also contains an explanation of why the program has been . . . well, discontinued."

"Does anyone have any specific questions at this time?" I asked the group.

Sarah Michigan raised her hand. I said, "Yes, Sarah?"

"What reason, if any, did the government give for stopping the program?"

"Good question," I said, "I should point out, we just found out about this ten minutes ago." I recounted what Carl had just explained to me.

Jake McGuire asked, "When will they start the bounty program? Do you have any idea?"

I said, "At this point, I'm unsure. It could start any day now. I can guarantee one thing. The minute it begins, I'll be out there taking down as many of those rot bags as possible. As far as I know, there will be no limit as to how many we can kill, and at $100 a pop, we can make a lot more money a lot faster than we could have made as part of Alpha Team, and each of you has been well trained to do just that."

I looked over at Carl, who was nodding in agreement.

He took a step forward, now feeling a bit more confident, and said, "Ladies and gentlemen. Allow me to express how sorry I am about all of this personally. But as Death Bringer Jones himself has just pointed out, you are all skilled zombie slayers now and should be able to make a decent enough living once the Dead Kill program begins."

"Dead Kill?" Sarah asked, and Carl explained how the program got its strangely accurate nickname.

Then from out in the crowd, Bill Jenkins said, "Too bad we didn't learn this before we went out there this morning. If so, maybe Jensen might still be alive."

I took a deep breath, prepared for my final speech to my trainees, and said, "I'm not even going to try to dispute that, Bill, because you're right, at least for today. However, what I will say is this. Those who decide to participate in this so-called Dead Kill program will face what happened to Joe Jensen every time we walk or drive out those gates and enter the outlands. Sure, there's lots of potential money to be made, but there is also the danger of having a repeat of what happened today.

"And being shot or killed is probably a lot better than being wounded or captured by Outlanders. We've all heard the stories of rape, torture, and, yes, even cannibalism among these animals. This danger will be present if you go out as part of a team or go it alone, as I plan on doing. There is a lot of money to be made during these zombie wars. But there's also a lot more danger. Also, keep in mind. As I told you during your training, the US army is also hunting and killing zombies and Outlanders. So, it's just as easy for any of us to be mistakenly shot and killed by fire from our soldiers, assuming we were Outlanders. I'm not trying to dissuade you in any way; I'm just stating the facts as I see them. This will be my final warning to you all; please, please be careful out there. Remember your training, and best of luck to you all."

With that, I turned to Carl, who handed me the envelopes. One by one, I called the trainee's name on the outside of the envelope, and when each approached, I shook their hand and handed them their final pay. It all went very quickly, and each of them acknowledged me, then turned and walked out the door. Some of them I would never see again; some I would encounter in the future. But regardless, I would do my best to keep tabs on them.

As for me, it looked like Sergeant Cruz was right about me once again, old lone wolf Jones.

EPILOGUE

So that's how my first year of the zombie apocalypse shook out. As I prepared to begin the second, I did so independently with no army, no Systematic Expansion team, no cohorts in crime, just me, myself, and I. As Carlton Elders had suggested, I kept the name Death Bringer, as well as the costume. I had gotten used to wearing it and made a few modifications to the original design.

I kept in touch with Carl and his son, Jack, and speaking of young Jack Elders; he continued to develop those comics based on stories I'd tell him. As the popularity of his comics grew, so did my fame. But I'm getting ahead of myself here. It's probably best if I save that for another day. Everything in this book occurred between 2043 and 2044, and it's now 2054. So, I have over a decade of stories to share with you, assuming I can find the time to write more and assuming you want to hear more.

I've got a new project in the works. Over the past 12 years, the Z43 virus has begun to mutate. Right now, the stories I've heard have only been unsubstantiated rumors. From what I've heard, it appears the only place these reported mutations occur has been in the outlands, where people continue to live like savage animals with poor sanitation and virtually no healthcare. Only now, all these years since the first year I've documented here, the outlanders have become barely human. It's no wonder the virus has evolved, and a whole new breed of monsters has arisen. But again, that's a story for another day. If I keep writing these stories with one year represented by one book, that new adventure will occur around book twelve. That is assuming I survive what I have planned. Otherwise, it will be up to someone else to chronicle my adventures.

I suppose time will tell.

DEATH BRINGER JONES'S ZOMBIE SLAYER RULES AS OF APRIL 2044

#1: Kill the head to kill them dead

#2: There's no time for wasting time

#3: It's no longer your bud when it rises from the mud.

#4: Fire first. Don't bother asking questions.

#5: Step on the gas, and flatten his ass.

www.ingramcontent.com/pod-product-compliance
Lightning Source LLC
Chambersburg PA
CBHW020337260626
47156CB00004B/1571